Anonymous

The Pacific Railroad Company

SALZWASSER
VERLAG

Anonymous

The Pacific Railroad Company

Reprint of the original, first published in 1859.

1st Edition 2023 | ISBN: 978-3-37514-122-6

Verlag (Publisher): Salzwasser Verlag GmbH, Zeilweg 44, 60439 Frankfurt, Deutschland
Vertretungsberechtigt (Authorized to represent): E. Roepke, Zeilweg 44, 60439 Frankfurt, Deutschland
Druck (Print): Books on Demand GmbH, In de Tarpen 42, 22848 Norderstedt, Deutschland

THE

PACIFIC RAILROAD COMPANY

OFFERS AT PUBLIC SALE

125,421 $\frac{76}{100}$ ACRES OF SELECTED

Farming, Timbered and Mineral Lands,

SITUATED IN THE COUNTIES OF

St. Charles, Jefferson, Washington, Franklin and Crawford,

ON BOTH SIDES OF

MAIN LINE AND SOUTH-WEST BRANCH

OF

PACIFIC RAILROAD,

In Tracts of 40 Acres & Upwards.

———

TERMS — 1-4th Cash, balance in 1, 2 & 3 years—Equal instalments, bearing 6 per cent. interest.

———

SALE TO COMMENCE

MONDAY, OCTOBER 3, 1859,

AT COURT HOUSE IN ST. LOUIS CITY.

———

ST. LOUIS, MO.

GEORGE KNAPP & CO., PRINTERS AND BINDERS.

1859.

PACIFIC RAILROAD FREE LANDS.

125,421 $\frac{71}{100}$ ACRES.

The Pacific Railroad offers for sale at Public Auction to the highest bidder, that portion of the Lands granted by the United States to the State of Missouri, by the Act of Congress June 10th, 1852, and by the State of Missouri to the Pacific Railroad, by Act of the General Assembly of Missouri, Dec. 25th, 1852, applicable to the construction of the main line of the Pacific Railroad, and known as the Pacific Railroad Free Lands.

All the conditions stipulated in the Act of Congress and the Act of the General Assembly of the State of Missouri having been fulfilled on the part of the Pacific Railroad, the title to the *Free Lands* can no longer be affected by *legislation.*

These Lands are situated in the Counties of St. Charles, Jefferson, Washington, Franklin and Crawford, on both sides of the main line of the Pacific Railroad as far as Franklin Depot, and of the South-west Branch as far as four sections deep in Range 2 West of the 5th Principal Meridian. They embrace Farming, Timbered and Mineral Lands.

FARMING LANDS.

The Farming Lands are peculiarly adapted to the culture of Tobacco, Wheat, Corn, and the different varieties of Grasses. They are all abundantly supplied with Timber, fine quarries of building Rock and Water.

They are located on the lines of the Pacific Railroad and South-west Branch, (Railroads now in operation,) all within fifteen miles of the Railroad, and none more than six hours distant by Rail from the City of St. Louis, the great Western Market for Agricultural products. Many of these lands are admirably adapted to the culture of the Grape and every variety of Fruit, and the success of those persons engaged in such pursuits indicates the counties in which these lands are located, as destined to be the great productive fruit lands of the West. Many of the tracts of land offered have already improvements upon them of considerable extent, enabling the purchasers at once to enter upon the culture of the land.

TIMBERED LANDS.

The Timbered Lands are the most desirable investment in the State; upon them is found every variety of Oak, Hickory, Ash, Elm, &c. They also embrace a portion of the Pineries of Washington County. The contiguity of these lands to the Railroad, covered with immense forests of the various kinds of timber used in the manufactories of St. Louis, gives them peculiar value, and should attract the attention of all the manufacturing interests requiring abundant and accessible supplies of choice timber. The great demand for fuel, each year increasing with the growth of the City of St. Louis, must ultimately be supplied from the lands along these Railroads.

The Pine Lands are a portion of the Indian Creek Pineries; they are well set with trees suitable for the saw, and will turn out the best qualities of lumber. They are so located as to command easy access to the South-west Branch, giving the owner the advantage of the St. Louis market, one of the finest Lumber Markets in the West.

MINERAL LANDS.

The Mineral Lands cover one of the largest and richest Mineral sections of the State, the Counties of Jefferson, Washington, Franklin, and Crawford, being unsurpassed in mineral wealth, each year yielding large quantities of both Lead and Iron to the parties operating the mines. Many of the tracts of land offered are known to have rich deposits of Lead, Iron and Copper upon them, and a portion of them are now worked, yielding large quantities of lead.

These lands must commend themselves to the attention of the capitalist seeking a safe and certain remunerative investment; for the amount of capital and labor employed in this Rich Mineral Region, the return in actual profits has been greater than in any other mineral section of the State.

The locality of the Virginia Mines, Darby Mines, Skewcs & Vallé Cove Mines, Mount Hope Mines, Thomas' Mines, Herrington Mines, Mineral Hill, Weins' Diggings, Williams' Mines, Evans' Lode, Hamilton Mines, Berthold Diggings—all Lead Mines; and Stanton Copper Mines, Heirch's Copper Mines, Park's Copper Mines, and numerous others within the boundaries of the Free Lands of the Pacific Railroad, is, of itself, sufficient to satisfy all that the sale of these lands should command the attention of every one desirous of securing a part of the wealth known to exist in this Rich Mineral Region.

A Map of the entire body of the lands has been prepared, showing the exact locality of each tract, with reference to the Railroad, County Seats, County Roads, Streams, &c.

A Catalogue of the Lands, giving the Section, Township, Range and Area, and abstract from Examiner's Report of the Lands, has been carefully prepared, and will furnish reliable information, in a general form, of the quantity and quality of land in each section.

The lands will be offered in the order in which they appear in the Catalogue, commencing for each County on the day designated, and continuing the sale from day to day until all the lands are offered.

All the lands offered have been examined and classified by the Land Agent of the Company; and his Township Plats and descriptive notes of each tract, furnishing accurate and reliable information concerning them, will at all times be accessible to parties seeking information in regard to the lands at the Land Office of the Pacific Railroad in the City of St. Louis.

TIME OF SALE.

The sale will take place at the Court-House, in the City of St. Louis, as follows:

Lands in St. Charles County, on Monday,　　Oct. 3d, 1859.
"　" Jefferson　　"　" Wednesday, " 5th, "
"　" Washington,　"　" Tuesday,　" 11th, "
"　" Franklin,　"　" Monday,　" 17th, "
"　" Crawford,　"　" Friday,　" 21st, "

TERMS:

The terms upon which these Lands are offered are as follows:

　　¼　Cash,
　　¼　in　one year;
　　¼　"　two years;
　　¼　"　three years.

The deferred payments bearing six per cent. interest per annum, secured by note and trust deed.

A discount of 10 per cent. allowed where the whole purchase money is paid down.

All purchasers at the time of bidding off a tract will be required to deposit ten dollars of the purchase money with the Auctioneers.

　　　　　　　　　　JOHN D. STEVENSON,
　　　　　　　　　　Land Agent Pacific Railroad.

BELT & PRIEST,
S. V. PAPIN & BRO.,　} *Auctioneers.*

G. C. SWALLOW,

State Geologist.

MINERALS.

The mineral wealth of the region under consideration is very great, and cannot fail, when fully developed, to command the admiration of the world, and greatly increase the material wealth of our State.

LEAD.

" *Crawford County.*—The 3d Magnesian Limestone in portions of this county is highly galeniferous. It is frequently characterized by vertical fissures and caverns, some of them of considerable size.

" *Lead Mines, Mineral Hill*, Sec. 32, T. 40, R. 2. W., examined by Mr. Englemann. The hill extends from N.E. of Sec. 32 to the N.E. of Sec. 33. The formation here is the 3d Magnesian Limestone, which is covered with a thick deposit of red clay. The whole side of the hill is marked with shallow diggings, from which immense quantities of ore have been obtained. These mines have been known for more than twenty years—upwards of 1,000,000 pounds of ore has been raised here, and as many as 500 men have been engaged in mining at one time. The mining has all been confined to surface diggings. East of this place, in Sec. 33, is a crevice containing a vein of lead five inches thick, adhering in a vertical sheet to the Magnesian Limestone. In N.E. of N.E. qr. of the same section, lead has been raised.

"*Williams' Mines*, located west of Mineral Hill, in Sec. 32, T. 40, R. 2, were opened in 1851, and up to April, 1854, the amount of ore raised was 202,183 pounds. During the remainder of 1854 there were raised 145,000 pounds. The course of the line of shafts and tunnels bears N.E. and S.W. The mineral was first procured 25 feet below the surface, and the deepest workings were 75 feet below the surface. The mineral is found in fissures of irregular dimensions, varying from two to eight feet in width, and three to four in height. It occurs in veins ranging through red clay, associated with brown hematite, pyrites and ochre. These mines have not been worked to any extent during the last three years.

"Nearly every portion of Secs. 32, 33, and 34, T. 40, R. 2 W., contains more or less lead. In the N.E. qr. of Sec. 1, T. 40, R. 2, there have been raised 10,000 pounds of ore.

"*Wein's Diggings* are located in S.E. of S.E. qr., Sec. 3, T. 38, R. 2 W. During the winters of 1856 and 1857 about 135,000 pounds of ore was raised.

"*Murtrey's Diggings* are situated north of Wein's Diggings, in the same section. A great deal of ore has been obtained here from surface diggings; but no mining has been done lately. On S.E. qr. of S.E. qr., T. 37, R. 2. W., about 200 pounds have been obtained from shallow diggings.

"*Halbert's*, in S.E. Sec., T. 37, R. 4. In 1844 from 3,000 to 4,000 pounds were obtained here from surface diggings.

"*Evans'*, in N.E. of Sec 3, T. 37, R. 3. In 1856 about 300 pounds were obtained from surface diggings.

"*Ransom's Mines*, (examined by Mr. Englemann,) in Sec. 15, T. 38, R. 2 W. The ore is found in the upper part of the 3d Magnesian Limestone. The mineral is supposed to occur in horizontal sheets, connecting with pockets. About 54,000 pounds of mineral have been obtained here, but no regular mining has been done.

"*Hinch's Mines*, in Sec. 3, T. 38, R. 2. About 500 or 600 pounds of ore have been obtained here. Lead has also been found in many places in this neighborhood.

"*Trask and Garrison's Mines*, near the middle of west line of Sec. 5, T. 36, R. 2 W., have yielded from 10,000 to 15,000 pounds of mineral.

"*Isgrig's Mines*, S.E. of N.E. qr. Sec. 4, T. 39, R. 2 W. A little surface digging has been done here.

"*Sappington's Mines*, N.W. qr. Sec. 1, T. 36, R. 2, were opened in the spring of 1857, since which time they have yielded 55,000 pounds of mineral.

"*Clark's Mines*, in same section, opened in 1853, have yielded 25,000 pounds.

"*Darby's Mines*, also in same section, were opened in 1855. They have been but little worked, and have yielded 7,000 pounds of ore. The last three mines are situated on the same hill, and were examined by Mr. Englemann. The ore occurs in small crevices and pockets, in Magnesian Limestone, and disseminated as float-mineral in red clay, and sometimes adhering to masses of sulphuret and brown oxide of iron.

"*Railroad* or *Coffee Diggings* are located on a spur of the same ridge, in S.W. qr. of Sec. 36, on Pacific Railroad land. Mining was commenced here in 1857, and 5,000 or 6,000 pounds have been raised.

"*Rutledge's Mines*, N.E. qr. Sec. 21, T. 39, R. 2, have been occasionally worked with good success.

"*Red Hills Mines*, N.E. of S.W. qr. Sec. 23, T. 4, R. 2. About 400,000 pounds of lead have been obtained, mostly from the red clay. A few small veins have been discovered in the underlying Magnesian Limestone.

"*Hibler's Diggings*, in N.E. of N.W. qr., Sec. 35, T. 40, R. 2 W. About 10,000 pounds of ore have been obtained. These mines have only been worked irregularly. The ore occurs in float-mineral, in the clay, in crevices and pockets, and in the form of thin sheets penetrating the Magnesian Limestone. Lead in small quantities has also been obtained in Secs. 26 and 27, T. 40, R. 2 W.

"All the above mentioned mines occur in 3d Magnesian Limestone. Lead has also been found at many places in 2d Magnesian Limestone, but only in small quantities.

"*Carbonate of Lead* occurs in small particles at William's Mines and at Mineral Hill.

"*Vallé and Skewes' Mines*.—These are the Cove Mine and Short Lode, on the north, and the Mount Hope Mine, on the south side of the Meramec.

" *The Cove Mine and the Short Lode* are in township 42 N.,
R. 1 E., Sec. 22, N.W. qr. They are on the side of a high
ridge, the height of which is about 200 feet above the level of
the valley. This ridge is capped with about fifty feet of sandstone, the lower portion of which is interstratified with Magnesian Limestone, and beneath which, so far as explored, are
heavy-bedded magnesian limestones, intermixed with chert and
quartz.

" At the *Cove Mine*, the galena is found in a vertical fissure, whose average width is not over six inches, the course of
which is N. 5° E., and with a slight inclination of seven inches
to the fathom to the east. This fissure has never yet been
found to widen out much over the above average width, but
preserves a nearly uniform course and width, so far as explored.
This fissure is sometimes filled entirely with galena; at other
points, this is accompanied by heavy spar and calc spar; and
sometimes these last, with clay, fill it completely.

" The main shaft is about 150 feet deep, at the head of which
is a fine exposure of sandstone that extends up to the top of
the ridge. South of this, sixty feet, is the bluff shaft, 132 feet
deep; and south of this are three other shafts, varying from
eighty-eight to fifty feet in depth, and distant from each other
from thirty to fifty-eight feet.

" South of main shaft, three levels have been run, connecting with the different shafts; and north, but two have been
cut, at a depth from each other of 101 feet into the hill, and
extending northwardly to a distance from the main shaft of
over 200 feet. Much of the ground has been stoped away
from main shaft, south to the Scott shaft, between the first and
second levels, and also between the same levels, north of the
main shaft. Above the first level, and north of the main
shaft, the fissure has been followed up into the sandstone, and
has been found well filled with mineral, which, at the time
of my visit, was yielding a large quantity of galena. This is not
an unimportant part, for though the results of observation in
other mining countries would teach us to anticipate a change in
the character and productiveness of a vein, in passing from one
rock into another of a totally different character, here, at least,
is one fact tending to show that the presence of sandstone was

not incompatible with the deposition of the galena, and that, perhaps, it is a too hasty generalization to conclude that our lead deposits are only productive within the limits of the magnesian limestones. The mineral is remarkably pure, and among the many specimens examined I found no intermixture with other ores.

" East of Cove Mine 120 yards, and on the same ridge, is another fissure called the Negro Lode. On it have been sunk, on the south side, three or four shafts, the deepest of which is fifty or sixty feet. Its course is nearly N. 10° W. But little work has been done by the present proprietors.

" Two hundred feet east of the Negro Lode is, apparently, another fissure, and running nearly parallel with it. Nothing has been done towards exploring it, excepting to dig some few shallow shafts on the hill side. It is called the Scott Lode.

" *Short Lode.*—This lode is 300 feet east of the Scott, about 280 yards east of the Cove Mine, and on the same hill with them. The lead is found here in fissure, that varies from one inch to two and a half feet in width. Its course is nearly north and south, being nearly parallel with the preceding. The fissure is vertical, and contains, in addition to the ore, the heavy spar, which most frequently accompanies the galena in this fissure. The lead ore is accompanied, sometimes, by sulphuret of zinc. Frequently, cubes of the galena are found encrusted with crystals of the carbonate of lead.

" A considerable amount of systematic mining has been done here. Three shafts—one, ninety feet; one, eighty-five feet; and another seventy-seven feet, have been sunk: levels at three different depths have been run, and the quantity of stoping has been considerable. It has been, and is still, worked with profit.

" On this ridge, which belongs to the third Magnesian Limestone, are three or four fissures passing down perpendicularly, with a course varying but little from due north and south, and containing galena as far down as they have been explored. They cover a belt of about 300 yards east and west, and though neither on the top nor on the side of the ridge is there scarcely any natural indication of their existence, they are found, under ground, preserving a uniform course to the north, and one has been traced and worked in this direction nearly 800 feet.

"As we pass directly south from the Cove Mine, we travel through the valley of the Meramec, and at a distance of about half a mile we come to a lone, isolated hill, which, from its total disconnection with all others, and its solitary appearance, has been denominated the Lost Hill. This has a height nearly equal to that of the ridge in which the above mines are situated, and in this it is reported that galena has also been found. After leaving the Lost Hill, and travelling nearly due south, we cross the Meramec, and in the bluffs on the south side we again find explorations for lead ore, nearly on a due south line and about two and a half or three miles from Cove Mine.

" *Evans' Lode.**—The first point we reach on this ridge, at which mining has been carried on, is what is known by the name of Evans' Lode. The galena is found here, also, in a vertical fissure, which has a width at some points of two feet. Its course is nearly north and south. It is filled with clay, sulphate of baryta and mineral, and the galena is frequently intermixed with sulphuret and carbonate of zinc. The mining here extends over a distance of 400 feet north and south, and seven shafts, varying from thirty-eight to one hundred and twenty feet, have been sunk, but three of which, however, are connected with levels. The work has not been so systematical nor so regular as at the preceding mines, and this it is reasonable to suppose would be the case, inasmuch as it has not been worked by the proprietor, but has been leased to different parties.

" By Mr. Evans I am informed that it has yielded about 200,-000 pounds of mineral.

" *Mount Hope Mine.*—Farther south and almost joining the above, and not improbably a continuation of it, is the Mount Hope Mine. They are both in the same ridge, the geological character of which is the same as that of the Cove Mine.

" The lead ore is here also found in a vertical fissure, the width of which varies from one inch to two feet. Its course is a little east of north and west of south, with a very slight inclination to the east. Sometimes it is filled entirely with a sheet

---

* For a further account of this and Casswell Mine, see p. 18.

of galena, and at other points it is found to contain, with lead ore, clay and heavy spar. The ore is sometimes accompanied with the carbonate and the sulphuret of zinc.

"About thirteen shafts have been sunk, varying from twenty feet to one hundred and thirty-three feet in depth. Most of them have been connected by levels, and the mining has extended over a line of nearly 800 feet, north and south.

"Among the debris brought up from the lowest levels at Mount Hope and Cove Mines were some few well-preserved Pleurotomaria and Euomphalus, and one of the most perfect of these last was almost directly in contact with galena.

" The galena found in this mine is accompanied, at some points, with the carbonate and sulphuret of zinc.

" The ore obtained from the Mount Hope, the Short, and the Cove Mines, has been all smelted, since the commencement of operations by the present company in 1849, in a rude reverberatory furnace in the neighborhood of the Cove, and no separate account has been kept of the yield of each mine. The quantity of lead made from 1849 to October of the present year (1854), according to the statement furnished me by Mr. Wm. Skewes, has been 1,947,780 pounds, all the ore having been obtained from the above mines of the company, and the greater part from Mount Hope Mine. The average number of hands employed has been between twenty and twenty-five.

"A blast furnace is now being erected, with which it is intended to smelt the very large quantity of slag that has been accumulating since the company obtained possession of the mines, and which will increase considerably the total amount of lead obtained from these mines during the last five years.

" *Virginia Mine.*—Some two or three miles nearly due south of Mount Hope is the famous Virginia Mine, on the 16th section, in township 41, and range 1 east. This mine was discovered in 1834 or 1835, by Bartlett Brundage, and the fame of it soon attracted to it a number of miners, who obtained the privilege of working lots of twenty-four feet in diameter; and during the first year of its discovery the number engaged in mining is supposed to have been between 200 and 300. The School Commissioners (for it was on the public school land), in order to secure the rent on the mineral obtained, determined to appoint a single smelter, who should be responsible for it; and the number of applicants was so great, that they decided to make the selection by the drawing of lots, when it fell to John Williamson, who, having held it for a short time, sold to C. B. and I. Inge for $7,000. They having retained this office until the autumn of 1835 or '86, disposed of their right for $14,000 to Mr. Clendennin. He held it for about one year, when the mineral having accumulated in such quantities that he could not or did not smelt as fast as it was brought in by the miners, great dissatisfaction was excited, and the miners having rebelled and refused to furnish him the mineral, suit was commenced, the final termination of which was that the lease granted to him was broken. Soon after a number of smelters were appointed by the Trustees of the Public Schools, and at one time there were as many as ten log and three ash furnaces in operation.

"In 1844, the Meramec Company obtained a lease for working the mine and smelting the mineral, with the understanding that they were to buy the miners' rights to the tracts on the lode. They commenced operations actively and energetically, putting up a steam engine and pump, sinking the shafts deeper, running levels, and erecting a furnace; when one of the parties becoming embarrassed in his mercantile business, and another dying, operations were suspended, in 1846, for the want of funds; and since that time little or nothing has been done, while the machinery has been rusting, the buildings decaying, and the shafts and levels been caving in.

"The ore is found more in a vertical fissure, whose course is nearly due north and south, and has been traced by diggings from a short distance north of the Meramec, over a line, extending northwardly into the Bennett tract, of not less than one mile in length. The fissure varies in width from one to fifteen feet; and at one point, at which it is still visible from the top of the shaft, is not less than two feet wide. The rock is covered with a thick, heavy bed of ferruginous clay, the average thickness of which is fifty feet, beneath which is some ten or twelve feet of cherty limestone, and below this is the magnesian limestone. The fissure is filled with clay, heavy spar, (some of which was well crystallized, mostly, however, amorphous, with a light sky-blue color,) and with galena.

" From this section it will be seen that the shafts sunk were very numerous ; but, doubtless, before the possession of the mine by the Meramec Company, most of them were sunk without regard to any system or regular mining operations. After the company took possession, the mining was more systematic, and most of their labor was confined to the neighborhood of the engine and north shafts, each of which was sunk to a depth of about 260 feet. Levels were cut from north shaft, both north and south, the latter communicating with Duguid and Prior's shaft. Dr. King, in his report, says that between engine and north shaft there was a vast cavern, extending from the first level connecting these two shafts, almost to the surface of the ground, with an average breadth of nearly five feet, and from fifty to one hundred feet in height, nearly filled with pure galena ; and that in the engine shaft, at the depth of 260 feet, the lode was as large and distinct as it generally was throughout the shaft.

" Before the operations of the Meramec Company, the mining was carried on at different points by different parties, acting without regular system, and the one independently of the other. Most of the mineral, I doubt not, was then obtained from comparatively shallow depths. How much of this fissure has been worked out along its course, so far as yet explored, and to the depth of the deepest shafts, I have no sufficient data to enable me to judge; but from the best information I have been enabled to obtain of the levels and the stoping, I should deem it an exaggerated estimate to place it at one-half.

" Of the total amount of mineral obtained here, it is, perhaps, impossible at present to obtain any true and accurate statement. Dr. King, who had an opportunity, about ten years ago, of examining the books of the School Trustees, found the total amount on which rent had been charged and paid, to be 4,610,-158 pounds ; but neither he nor any one else supposes that this was all that, up to that time, had been obtained.

"Among all the estimates I have obtained from those who were familiar with the operations at this mine, there is none less than 8,000,000 pounds; some 15,000,000 pounds; but the majority of them place it at 10,000,000 pounds of ore.

"However great may seem the above estimate, I do not

doubt, had shafts been sunk systematically, levels been run at suitable and required depths, machinery been erected to keep the mine dry, and the ground been stoped away with any thing like scientific and practical skill, that the Virginia Mine would have been more productive than it has been, and, instead of lying idle, would be still yielding a handsome interest on the investment.

"For many of the above facts, in regard to the Virginia Mine, I am indebted to the Rev. Mr. Clarke and Mr. I. Nash Inge.

"*Darby's Mine*, in Town. 41 N., R. 1 W., Sec. 20, S.E. qr. This mine was worked some four or five years ago, and, according to all reports, with considerable profit. Operations were suspended on account of the water, but lately a new lease has been obtained by Mr. Giles, who is now engaged in working it.

"This mine is in the spur of a magnesian limestone hill. A shaft has been sunk fifty-two feet deep, and an adit cut for the purpose of drainage. At the bottom of this shaft a level has been run thirty feet, nearly east and west, and near this was found a large cave (denominated by the miners, chimney), extending nearly to the surface of the hill, and which was found filled with clay, tumbling rock, and a considerable quantity of mineral.

"The quantity of water (which is removed by pump, worked by horse power) is so great, that it is necessary to keep the present pump in constant operation, night and day ; and, this having been intermitted for several days previous to my visit, I found the shaft filled with water to nearly the adit level.

"Specimens of the mineral seen from this mine were tolerably massive, much of it crystallized in cubes, the sides of many of which were coated with crystals of the carbonate of lead. At the bottom of the shaft were found considerable quantities of the yellow iron pyrites, intermixed with sulphuret of zinc.

"Mr. Giles reports, that during the seven months he has been working, with the assistance of seven hands more than half the time, and during the remainder with that of only four hands, he has obtained 8,000 pounds of mineral. The estimated amounts of mineral, obtained from this mine, anterior to Mr.

Giles' lease, varies from 100,000 to 126,000 pounds of mineral.

"*Elliott Mine*, in Town. 41 N., R. 1 W., Sec. 6. This mine lies on the south-western extremity of a ridge, the course of which is a little west of north, and east of south. According to Dr. Shumard, the top of the hill is sandstone, beneath which is the third magnesian limestone.

"The only mineral obtained here has been from the clay, on the side of the hill, one acre of which is almost entirely covered with shallow shafts, the deepest I found open being twenty-one feet. The mineral obtained has been principally from three ranges, the general course of which was N.E. and S.W., running parallel with one another, and distant fifteen to twenty feet from each other. The exposure in the shafts was a reddish ferruginous clay, varying from twelve to twenty feet, below chert, and beneath this the tumbling magnesian limestone. The average depth of the shafts is not over twelve feet, and the deepest ever sunk was forty feet.

"The mineral is a very pure galena, accompanied by neither calc spar nor heavy spar, and exhibits not the least intermixture with either iron or zinc ores. As yet, it has been found only in the clay and chert. Work was commenced here in June, 1853; and since then, with six hands, it is reported that 70,000 pounds of mineral has been obtained.

Besides the above, there are quite a number of points in Franklin county at which galena has been obtained, and, at some of them, in considerable quantities, but which were not worked during the times of my visits to that county in 1853 and 1854. Most of them were not visited; and I subjoin a list of them, with the amounts of mineral which were reported to me as having been obtained.

"On the school section in Town. 42 N., R. 1 W., in 1827 and '28, there had been considerable digging. The mineral was found in the clay. The deepest shafts were about fifty feet. The diggings extended over an area of nearly ten acres, but did not extend down into the rock. Mr. A. Chambers, who worked these, obtained and smelted during the above years 40,000 pounds of mineral, and estimates the amount obtained at other times, and hauled to other furnaces, at 25,000 pounds.

2

" The *Hamilton Mines,* Town. 42 N., R. 1 W., Sec. 31, have not been worked for the last six years. The digging was confined to the clay, and the amount of mineral reported to have been obtained was 100,000 pounds.

"At *Massey's Mine,* Town. 41 N., R. 1 W., Sec. 14, one shaft had been sunk sixty feet, but most of the other shafts were not over twelve feet. Up to October, 1853, Mr. Massey estimated the amount of mineral obtained at from 2,000 to 3,000 pounds. They are much incommoded by water at these diggings.

" *Berthold* and *Generally's Diggings* are near Mitchel's creek, in Sec. 13, Town. 41 N., R. 1 W. They are principally on the side of a hill. The deepest shaft was fifty-four feet, and which was filled with water at the time of my visit, in October, 1858. Mr. Generally gave, as the total amount of mineral obtained here, 100,000 pounds."

" The *Casswell Mine.*—Since the foregoing report was written, I have had the pleasure of visiting this valuable mine in company with the Hon. John F. Darby, one of the proprietors. It is situated on the N. ½ of the S.W. qr. Sec. 34, T. 42, R. 1. E., in the bluff of the southern side of the Meramec. At the mine the bluff rises rather abruptly to the height of some 200 feet. The rocks at the base are the upper beds of the 3d Magnesian Limestone, and those cropping out on the brow of the hill, near the top, are the lower beds of the 2d Sandstone.

The vein was discovered in the fall of 1855 by Mr. Brewer, who opened the mine and raised about 12,000 pounds of galena. It was next worked by Mr. Erie Standifer, who took out some .15,000 pounds of the ore. Mr. Michael Dolan has worked it, from time to time since 1856 under the direction of the present owners, Messrs. Darby, Vandeventer and Beardslee, and has raised about 100,000 pounds of good galena.

Mr. Dolan's systematic operations very clearly indicate the characters and value of the vein. It cuts through the bluff in a direction nearly north and south, and almost perpendicular, but inclining a little to the east in its descent. The lead ore is nearly all the sulphuret, though the carbonate sometimes occurs. The gangue is heavy spar, calc spar, and red clay. The thickness of the vein varies from two inches to ten. This vein, like the Evans, cuts through the lower beds. of the 2d Sandstone and down into the 3d Magnesian Limestone, which forms the base of the bluff. From a point on the slope near the base of the Sandstone a shaft has been sunk 95 feet into the limestone, and an adit has been run on the vein some 200 feet from near the base of the bluff, intersecting the shaft above named. The appearance, position and direction of this vein seem to indicate that it is a continuation of the Evans Lode,* on the south side of the ridge, which some have supposed to be a part of the Mount Hope vein.

Whether these veins shall prove to be one and the same, and whether they prove to be *true veins*, extending down indefinitely, or merely to the base of the formation in which they are found, they can not fail to be extensive and valuable. The length of the two is not less than one mile, and the average depth of the parts not worked, to the bottom of the 3d Magnesian Limestone, can not be less than 300 feet, and is probably between 400 and 500 feet.

In estimating the profits of mining on these veins, it will be safe to put down the length at one mile and the depth below the Sandstone at 400 feet, and that the remainder of the vein will prove as rich or even richer than the parts worked out. But these estimates are made upon the most unfavorable opinions respecting the character of these lead veins. The opinion expressed by some geologists that these are only *Gash-veins*, and confined to one formation, the 3d Magnesian Limestone, has no support in the appearance of the country or the character of the veins themselves. And I submit the proposition, with all due deference to the opinions of others, that no geologist can examine the phenomena presented by this vein, and the Evans Mine, and the Virginia Mine, and make them conform in any tolerable degree to the definition given of a *Gash-vein*. On the contrary, all the facts observed point most significantly to the characters of *true veins—veins* which extend downwards indefinitely, without regard to the limits of formations. With this view of the character of these veins,

---

* See page 12.

which I conceive to be the true one, the value of these and the neighboring mines will be vastly increased, as there will be no fear of exhausting them.

The unfavorable opinion respecting the Lead Mines of Missouri, which has prevailed to some extent among foreign miners and capitalists, has arisen, I apprehend, from the erroneous opinions of some geologists that our mines have characteristics and geological relations similar to those of the Wisconsin mines. While I shall not deny that some of our lead veins resemble those of Wisconsin, and appear like *Gash-veins*, there are many others in which the analogy does not hold good in any one important character.

1. According to Mr. Whitney, the valuable lead veins of Wisconsin are confined to a formation not more than 100 feet thick; but in Missouri the most valuable veins range through three formations, the aggregate thickness of which is not less than 1,000 feet.

2. In Wisconsin the lead veins are limited to one formation in the upper part of the Lower Silurian System, while in Missouri the most valuable veins range through two members of the Carboniferous system and the two lower formations of the Silurian.

3. While in Wisconsin, so far as I know, there are no evidences of extensive igneous action or violent disturbances in the neighborhood of the lead mines, in Missouri, both within and around the lead field, there are most decisive proofs of extensive igneous action and violent disturbances—mountains of granite and porphyry have been thrown up—mountains and ridges of porphyry have been fractured and rent asunder, and the fissures filled with dykes (veins) of granite, greenstone, quartz, basalt, dolerite and porphyry, and *true veins* of copper and wolfram, and veins (where the metalic ore fills the entire fissure) of specular iron and galena; some of these dykes pass into the sedimentary rocks, changing the sandstone to quartzite and the limestone (the lower lead-bearing beds) into crystalline marble.

4. In Wisconsin the profitable veins have not extended more than 100 feet in depth, but in Missouri two shafts have been

sunk on the large Virginia vein to the depth of 260 feet, without any diminution or indication that it would run out.

5. In Missouri some of the veins do pass from the limestone into the sandstone above, as seen at the Evans and the Caswell Mines.

6. Many of the veins in Missouri present all the appearances of *true veins;* dislocations and disturbances have been produced by powerful agencies, as indicated in some places by the fragments of the original strata filling a part of the fissure, by well marked and extensive slickensides, by the displacement of the strata, and the irregularity of the fissure.

7. The veins are often very long; some have been explored more than one mile.

8. In many mines the fissures are filled as they usually are in *true veins;* the sheet of galena runs through the middle, with a gangue of heavy spar or calc spar, or both, on each side.

9. Selvages, so remarkable in *true veins,* also occur in the Missouri mines.

Such are some of the facts which should lead us to suspect the validity of all arguments drawn from any apparent analogy between the Wisconsin mines and our own. And besides, even on the supposition that our veins do not extend below the base of the 3d Magnesian Limestone, there is still from 200 to 400 feet of this rock below the deepest workings of nearly all the mines in the counties of Jefferson, Franklin, Crawford, and the north of Washington; while in the South-west the lead-bearing portion of the Mountain Limestone is at least 200 feet thick. Below these beds are the Chemung rocks, which are not over 100 feet in thickness. Whether the lead passes down through this formation is not known, as no vein has been traced or worked to it. The character of the rock, however, does not indicate the existence of valuable veins, though some deposits of lead and copper have been discovered in it. In passing from the Chemung rocks near the northern boundary of Taney, we come directly upon the lead-bearing rocks of that county, which are the 2d and 3d Magnesian Limestones. The 1st and 2d Sandstones are very thin or entirely wanting in this part of the county, while the 2d and 3d Magnesian Limestones present an aggregate thickness varying from 600 to 1,000 feet.

These facts show that the mines of Newton and Jasper have beneath them at least 1,000 feet of lead-bearing limestones, and those in Taney from 600 to 800 feet of the lower part of the same beds. In view of these conclusions, based as they are upon the most unfavorable opinions entertained by any of the character of our veins, the miner and capitalist need not fear the exhaustion of our lead mines; but, when they take into consideration the facts above stated, which show an entire want of analogy between our own mines and those on the Upper Mississippi, and which point so conclusively to the most reliable characteristics of true veins, their fears, if any still exist, that our lead mines have seen their most prosperous days, must be banished, and they will continue their operations with brighter hopes of eminent success.

These views are fully sustained by the most recent developments of our mines, as some of the oldest have been reopened and worked with greater success than ever before; and besides the deepest diggings have often proved the most profitable.

While, then, it may be true that some of our lead deposits are only *Gash-veins*, others (and among them the Casswell) give every indication of being *true veins*.

COPPER.

Crawford County.

" The copper mines of Crawford county have not been worked for some years. Dr. H. King examined them at the time they were being worked, from whose report we largely avail ourselves.

" *Hinch's Copper Mines*, on the side of a hill, near the center of Sec. 4, T. 38, R. 2 W. This mine was discovered in 1849, and several thousand pounds of ore have been raised here. According to Dr. King, the ore, near the surface, is a carbonate and oxide, but deeper it assumes the character of a sulphuret of excellent quality. Dr. King states that 800 lbs. of ore produced 273 lbs. of good pig copper. The holes or shafts have been sunk chiefly in loose, red clay and comminuted chert, but the walls of some of them are in the Magnesian

Limestone. The copper ore was found with brown hematite in small fragments disseminated through the clay and filling fissures in sandstone. Small scales of native copper were found occasionally with the carbonate and oxide.

"Mr. Engelmann states that very little has been done here toward investigating the real character of this mine, owing to the very irregular manner in which the work has been carried on.

"*Bleeding Hill*, in S.W. of N.W. qr. Sec. 4, T. 38, R. 2 W., was examined by Mr. Engelmann. A few shallow shafts have been sunk here, chiefly through red clay and chert.

"The ore is found in small fissures in 2d Sandstone, and consists of green and blue carbonate, sulphuret, and some scales of virgin copper, commingled with a great deal of earthy brown hematite. No systematic mining has been done here, but much useless labor has been spent.

"In Sec. 22, T. 40, R. 2 W., some excavations have been made, but only small fragments of blue and green carbonate have been found. A few pieces have also been found on Huzza and Crooked creeks.

PARK'S COPPER MINE.

Washington County.

I am indebted to Mr. J. V. Phillips for a full report, illustrated with numerous sections and maps, upon the Copper Mine of Mr. Andrew Park, in Sec. 17, T. 40, R. 1 E., Washington county. I regret that I can not publish it in full, as it would not be intelligible without the sections. From it I make the following summary and extracts:

"The vein is in the upper part of the 3d Magnesian Limestone, and appears to run parallel with the strata, which dip about 10° toward the center of the ridge. It is seen on the sides of the ridge in several places for more than a mile in extent, and has been opened in three localities; in one, the level was extended fifty feet on the lode. The vein contains the green and blue carbonates and the yellow and gray sulphurets of copper, in a gangue of clay, heavy spar, calc spar and oxide of iron in cherty matter.

"Mr. Park, who had charge of the mining operations, thinks the vein showed a disposition to open out, about every eight feet, in vertical seams or crevices. These openings are filled with decomposed flint and ferruginous matter, and are about one foot wide.

"The ore in all the openings evidently belongs to the same vein, which is horizontal, and will doubtless follow the dip of the limestone to the center of the ridge; and each ridge may be supposed to form a *copper basin*, and the central basin to be the center from which these ridges radiate. The richest portion of the vein or deposit may be looked for near the center of the basin. There is evidently a large amount of copper ore in these basins, and it lies in a good position for economical mining."

About ten tons of the ore has been taken out; it yields about twenty per cent. of copper.

Mr. Phillips estimates the profits on every hundred tons of ore raised and shipped to Baltimore, at $5,950.

EXTRACT FROM DR. LITTON'S REPORT.

"*Stanton Copper Mine*, T. 40 N., R. 2 W., Sec 2, where mining was commenced by the present company, in 1851, and has been continued to the present date, without interruption.

"This mine is in the spur of a ridge, the course of which is about N., 70° E., terminating, at its eastern extremity, in a valley. In most places, this ridge is covered with soil, with now and then, on its top and sides, an exposure of rock. As we pass from its eastern extremity, along the top of it, we find no other rock than Magnesian Limestone, in place, until within 300 yards of the range of the shafts, where Sandstone is found both on the top and sides. At the eastern extremity of the ridge, the Magnesian Limestone is almost perfectly horizontal, with no perceptible dip, until it approaches the Sandstone, when it is seen dipping down for a short distance, at an angle of ten or fifteen degrees, to the west. This Sandstone continues west for about 600 feet, visible at points, both on the top and sides of the ridge; but no other rock was seen (excepting on the south side, and near its base, where Dr. Shumard measured a brecciated mass, eighteen feet high, consisting of chert and Magnesian Limestone, until passing a short distance west of the range of shafts, where the Magnesian Limestone was again visible, with, at first, a dip of ten or fifteen degrees to the east; but a short distance further west, on the same ridge, it was horizontal. In the Sandstone, whether exposed on the ridge, or examined in the driftings, I found no appearance of stratification. The surface of the ridge is so covered with soil, that it is impossible to examine the eastern and western junctions of the Sandstone with the Magnesian Limestone; but I infer, from examination of the driftings in the mine, that the western junction is irregular, with a general course across the ridge of about N., 20° W.; and that along this line, there is, in all probability, a space, for some distance beneath the surface, filled with the debris of the two rocks.

" Most of the mining done has been in a space, irregular, so far as explorations have shown, the direction of which is across and extending below the base of the ridge, and with a general course of about north, twenty degrees west, and of an estimated width of from forty to sixty feet, bounded on the east by Sandstone, and on the west by Magnesian Limestone. This, so far as explored, is found filled with tumbling rock, clay, chert, calc spar (semi-crystalline, and colored red by peroxide of iron), masses of iron ore and copper ores.

" From the vertical section, it will be seen that there are five shafts, the deepest of which (engine shaft) is 115 feet, and in which is the pump, worked by a steam engine. In sinking it, tumbling rock, of a magnesian character, was found through its entire depth, and it is cribbed from top to bottom. This shaft is connected by a level, 145 feet in length, with a shaft ninety feet deep, north of it, and thus connecting with the main works in the north hill. At the time of my last visit this level extended no farther than this shaft; but, since then, it has been run northwardly, the depth of about fifty feet below all preceding driftings; and, as I am informed by one of the company, with good success and fine prospects. Levels have been run into the north hill, from both the north and south sides; but most of the driftings have been fifty feet below these, and above which driftings, only (as represented on the vertical section), the ground has been stoped away.

"The copper ores found here are a mixture of the gray sulphuret and the green carbonate. Two analyses of a specimen, which was richer than the average run, gave the following results :—

	I.	II.
Silica,	1.16	1.29
Sulphur,	2.02	2.10
Peroxide of iron,	12.85	12.20
Oxide of copper,	61.16	60.16
Carbonic acid, water and loss,	22.81	24.25

Giving, as the mean of the two determinations, 48.41 per cent. of copper.

"The furnace for smelting the ore is distant from the mine about one mile, where there is an abundance of water during the whole year, for washing the ores, and supplying a blast for the furnace during eight months in the year. For this last purpose, however, the company have lately erected, at this point, a steam engine, and are now enabled to continue, at all seasons, their smelting operations. They are now engaged in smelting a large quantity of copper ore that has accumulated during the present year, and which, it is estimated, will produce thirty tons of copper; that, added to the twenty or thirty tons previously made, will make the total amount of copper made here, since the commencement of operations, in 1851, about fifty tons.

"During the first year of the operations of the Company, there was but little mining, most of the labor having been expended in erecting the furnace; and the average number of hands was not over six. During 1852, the average number of hands was about ten; and, at present, there are, probably, twenty or twenty-five in the employ of the company."

The owners deserve great credit for the energy with which they prosecuted the exploration of this mine, to prove the character of this and other copper deposits in the State.

TABLE OF LOCALITIES OF COPPER ORE.

The star (*) denotes the localities where the copper has been worked.

No. of Locality	Name of Mine.	Township.	Range.	Section.	County.	Whether on R.R. Land.	Kind of Ore.	Whether Worked.	By whom reported.	Remarks.
1	......	35	2 E	......	Washington	....	Carbonate and Sulphuret	....	Litton	5 m's east of Caledonia.
2	Jordan	36	3 & 4	1 & 6	Washington	....	....	....	Litton	....
3	Stanton	40	2 W	2	Franklin	....	Gray Sulphuret & green Carbonate	*	Litton	....
4	Silver Hollow	40	1 W	N.W. 8	Franklin	....	Gray Sulphuret & green Carbonate	not now	Litton	....
5	Hurst	41	1	26 & 27	Franklin	....	....	....	Shumard	....
6	......	41	1	34	Franklin	....	....	....	Shumard	....
7	Bredell	41	....	....	Franklin	....	....	....	Shumard	....
8	Copper Hill	40	2 W	24	Crawford	....	Gray Sulphuret, Red Oxide and Blue Carbonate,	not now	Litton	R.R. land in this section.
9	......	38	3 W	14	Crawford	....	....	....	Shumard	....
10	Reeves	39	3	13	Crawford	....	....	....	Shumard	....
11	Bleeding Hill	38	2	4	Crawford	....	Carbonate, Oxide, Sulphuret and Native.	not now	Engelmann	See Dr. King's report.
12	& Hinch's	38	2	......	Crawford	....	....	....	Engelmann	
13	......	36	4	22	Crawford	....	....	....	Shumard	....
14	Hibler	40	2	22	Crawford	....	Blue and Green Carbonate	*	Shumard	....
15	......	38	5	15	Crawford	....	....	....	Shumard	....
16	......	40	9 W	2	Maries	....	....	....	Broadhead	
17	......	30	24W	19	Green	....	Sulphuret	....	Broadhead	In Lower Encr. Limest.
18	Haralson	29	24	10	Green	R.	Sulphuret and green Carbonate	not now	Broadhead	Some found on R.R. land
19	......	29	25	2	Lawrence	....	Sulphuret	....	Broadhead	In Lower Encr. Limest.
20	Jos. Stogdill	30	25	S.E. N.E. 23	Dade	....	Sulphuret and green Carbonate	....	Broadhead	In F. f. and i.
21	Jos. Stogdill	30	25	S.W. N.W. 24	Dade	....	Sulphuret and green Carbonate	....	Broadhead	In Lower Encr. Limest.
22	......	29	24	2	Green	....	Sulphuret	....	Swallow	
23	......	....	....	....	Dallas	....	Sulphuret and Carbonate	....	Swallow	
24	Goose	26	19	S.E. 9	Taney	....	Sulphuret and Carbonate	....	Swallow	In Magn. Limestone.
25	......	....	....	......	Benton	....	Sulphuret	....	Swallow	

COPPER FURNACES.

| 1 | Stanton | 40 | 2 W | N.E. ¼ 1 | Franklin | .... | Copper | .... | not | Litton | Since 1851. Steam power. |

ST. CHARLES COUNTY.

6,869 $\frac{76}{100}$ Acres.

Sale commences MONDAY, October 3, 1859.

TOWNSHIPS.	Area. Acres	100ths.	DESCRIPTIVE NOTES.
45, *Range* 2 *East*.			
Section 4.			
E ½ of N.E. ¼	80		Upland, timbered; hickory, white and black oak; E. ½ of N.E. ¼ improvement.
S.W. ¼ of S.E. ¼	40		
W. ½ of S.W. ¼	80		
Section 6.			
E. ½ of section	321		Upland, timbered; hickory, white and black oak.
E. ½ of lots 1 & 2 of N.W. ¼	62	39	
Lot 2 of S.W. ¼	39	60	
Section 8.			
E. ½ of section	320		Upland, timbered; hickory, white and black oak.
W. ½ of S.W. ¼	80		
Section 10.			
E. fr. ½ of section	262	39	Upland, arable, timbered; hickory, white and black oak.
S. ½ of N.W. ¼	80		
Section 12.			
N.W. ¼ of N.E. ¼	40		Broken upland, good soil, well timbered, oak and hickory.
N.E. ¼ of N.W. ¼	38	25	
W. ½ of N.W. ¼	76	50	
Section 18.			
E. ½ of section	320		Thin upland, timbered, white and black oak.
S.W. fr. ¼	91	17	
Section 20.			
N. ½ of N.E. fr. ¼	75	55	Same.
N.W. ¼	160		
Section 28.			
N.W. fr. ¼	93	41	Same.
W. ½ of S.W. ¼	80		
Section 30.			
W. ½ and S.E. ¼ of S.E. ¼	120		Upland, well timbered, hickory and oak.
S. ½ of S.W. ¼	54	50	
Section 32.			
E. ½ of N.E. ¼	80		Thin upland, well timbered; white, black and post oak.
S.W. ¼ of N.W. ¼	40		
S. ½ of section	288	62	

TOWNSHIP.	Area Acres 100ths.	DESCRIPTIVE NOTES.
44, *Range* 2 *East*.		
Section 6.		
W. ½ of section	318 62	Broken, timbered, white and black oak.
N. ½ of N.E. ¼	80	
S.E. ¼	160	
Section 8.		
N. ½ of N.W. fr. ¼	61 71	Same.
45, *Range* 1 *East*.		
Section 2.		
S.E. ¼ of S.E. ¼	40	Same.
Section 10.		
S.E. ¼ of N.E. ¼	40	Same.
S.W. ¼ of S.W. ¼	40	
Section 12.		
E. ½ & S.W. ¼ of N.E. ¼	120	Same.
S. ½ of N.W. fr. ¼	74	
S. fr. ½ of section	208	
Section 14.		
S.E. ¼ of S.E. ¼	40	Same.
N. ½ of S.W. fr. ¼	73 25	
Section 20.		
S.W. ¼ of S.E. ¼	40	Thin upland, timbered; white and black oak, watered.
Section 24.		
N.W. ¼ of N.E. fr. ¼	27 99	Same.
S.W. ¼ of S.E. ¼	40	
S. ½ of S.W. ¼	80	
Section 26.		
N. ½ of N.E. ¼	80	Broken upland, soil thin, well timbered, hickory and oak.
N. ½ of N.W. ¼	80	
S.E. ¼ of S.E. ¼	40	
S.W. ¼ of S.W. ¼	40	
Section 28.		
W. ½ of section	320	Thin upland well timbered, white, black and post oak.
E. ½ of N.E. ¼	80	
N.W. ¼ of S.E. ¼	40	
Section 30.		
S.W. ¼ of N.E. ¼	40	Same.
S.E. ¼ of N.W. ¼	40	
Section 32.		
S.W. ¼	160	Same.
Section 34.		
W. ½ of N.E. ¼	80	Same.
S.E. ¼ of S.E. ¼	40	
N.W. ¼	160	
N. ½ of S.W. ¼	80	
Section 36.		
N. ½ of section	320	Broken upland, timbered with variety of oaks.
S.W. ¼	160	
N.W. ¼ of S.E. ¼	40	

TOWNSHIP.	Area. Acres 100ths.	DESCRIPTIVE NOTES.
44, *Range* 1 *East.*		
Section 2.		
N.E. ¼	160	Rough upland, oak timber.
N.W. ¼ of N.W. ¼	40	
Section 4.		
W. ½ of N.E. ¼	80	Part arable, timbered with white and black oak.
N.W. ¼ of S.E. ¼	40	
N.W. ¼	160	
E. ½ of S.W. fr. ¼	73 60	
Section 6.		
W. ½ of lot 2 of N.E. ¼	37 87	Same.
W. ½ of lot 2 of N.W. ¼	81 34	
Section 12.		
E. ½ of N.E. ¼	80	2d rate upland, timbered, oak and hickory.

JEFFERSON COUNTY.

36,571 $\frac{47}{100}$ Acres.

Sale commences WEDNESDAY, October 5, 1859.

TOWNSHIP.	Area. Acres 100ths.	DESCRIPTIVE NOTES.
43, *Range* 5 *East.*		
Section 14.		
S.W. fr. ¼	6 62	Thin upland.
Section 18.		
E. ½ & N.W. ¼ of S.E. ¼	80	
Lot 2 and N. ½ of lot 1 of S.W. ¼	130 20	
Section 20.		
E. ½ of N.W. ¼	80	Broken upland, some bottom well timbered; black, white and post oak; branch water.
W. ½ & S.E. ¼ of N.E. ¼	120	
E. ½ & S.W. ¼ of S.E. ¼	120	
S.W. ¼	160	
Section 22.		
S. ½ of N.W. ¼	80	Thin upland, well timbered, white and post oak, branch water.
Section 24.		
S. ½ of S.W. fr. ¼	79 55	Same.
Section 26.		
S.E. ¼ of N.E. ¼	40	Broken upland, well timbered, varieties of oak, branch water.
S.W. ¼ of N.W. ¼	40	
W. ½ of S.W. ¼	80	

TOWNSHIP.	Area. Acres 100ths.	DESCRIPTIVE NOTES.
Section 28.		
N.W. ¼ of N.E. ¼	40	Same.
E. ½ & N.W. ¼ of S.W. ¼	120	
Section 30.		
E. ½ & S.W. ¼ of S.E. ¼	120	Same.
Section 32.		
E. ½ of S.E. ¼	80	Same.
S. ½ of N.W. ¼	80	
42, *Range 5 East.*		
Section 2.		
S.E. ¼ of S.E. ¼	30 31	Thin upland, black and white oak.
Section 4.		
S. ½ of section	320	Broken upland, thin soil; black, white and post oak; well timbered.
E. ½ & S.W. ¼ of N.E. ¼	142 41	
E. ½ & N.W. ¼ of N.W. ¼	142 61	
Section 6.		
S.E. ¼ of N.E. ¼	40	Same.
E. ½ of S.E. ¼	80	
Lot 2 and W. ½ of lot 1 of N.W. ¼	92 50	
Section 8.		
N.E. ¼	160	Same.
E. ½ of N.W. ¼	80	
W. ½ & N.E. ¼ of S.E. ¼	120	
S.W. ¼	160	
Section 10.		
N.W. ¼ of N.E. fr. ¼	39 57	Rolling upland, well timbered—white, black and post oak—spring and branch water.
E. ½ & S.W. ¼ of N.W. ¼	120	
S. ½ of section	320	
Section 14.		
S.E. ¼ of N.E. ¼	40	Thin upland, broken, well timbered.
W. ½ & S.E. ¼ of N.W. ¼	120	
S.E. ¼	160	
E. ½ & N.W. ¼ of S.W. ¼	120	
Section 18.		
E. ½ of section	320	Same.
S.W. ¼	151 48	
Section 22.		
N.W. fr. ¼	7	Same.
N.W. ¼ of S.W. ¼	40	
E. ½ & S.W. ¼ of S.E. fr. ¼	82	
Section 28.		
E. ½ of section	320	Same.
E. ½ & S.W. ¼ of N.W. ¼	120	
S.W. ¼	160	
Section 30.		
N. ½ of section	305 57	Same.
S.E. ¼ & N.W. ¼ of S.E. ¼	80	
Lot 2 & N. ½ of lot 1 S.W. ¼	107	

TOWNSHIP.	Area. Acres 100ths.	DESCRIPTIVE NOTES.
Section 32.		
N.W. ¼ of N.W. ¼	40	Same.
E. ½ & S.W. ¼ of N.E. ¼	120	
S.E. ¼	160	
E. ½ & S.W. ¼ of S.W. ¼	120	
Section 34.		
N. ½ of N.W. fr. ¼	47 80	Same.
41, *Range* 5 *East.*		
Section 6.		
N. ½ of section	331 25	Rolling upland, well timbered; different varieties of oak.
Lot 2 of S.W. fr. ¼	29	
43, *Range* 4 *East.*		
Section 2.		
Lot 1 & E. ½ of lot 2 N.E. ¼	125	Upland, rolling, well timbered; black, white and post oak; 8 miles of railroad.
S.E. ¼	160	
Section 4.		
E. ½ of N.E. ¼	80 62	Same.
S. E. ¼	160	
W. ½ of section	318 36	
Section 8.		
N. fr. ½ of section	218 20	Same.
E. ½ & N.W. ¼ of S.E. ¼	120	
Section 10.		
W. ½ of N.W. ¼	80	Same.
S.E. ¼	160	
S.E. ¼ of S.W. ¼	40	
Section 12.		
N.W. ¼ of S.W. ¼	40	Same.
Section 14.		
W. ½ of N.E. ¼	80	Rolling upland, thin soil, well timbered; different varieties of oak.
E. ½ & S.W. ¼ of N.W. ¼	120	
S.W. ¼	160	
Section 20.		
W. fr. ½ and N.E. fr. ¼ of N. W. ¼	79 57	Upland and bottom, well timbered and watered; different kinds of oak.
Section 22.		
S. ½ of N.E. ¼	80	Broken uplands, thin soil, well timbered; varieties of oak; 6 miles of railroad.
S.E. ¼	160	
N. fr. ½ of S.W. ¼	41 76	
S. fr. ½ & N.W. ¼ of N.W. ¼	104 19	
Section 24.		
W. ½ & S.E. ¼ of N.E. ¼	120	Same.
S.W. ¼ of N.W. ¼	40	
S.E. ¼ of S.E. ¼	40	
S.W. ¼	160	
Section 26.		
E. ½ & N.W. ¼ of N.E. ¼	120	Same.
N.E. ¼ of N.W. ¼	40	

TOWNSHIP.	Area. Acres 100ths.	DESCRIPTIVE NOTES.
Section 30.		
S.W. ¼ of N.E. ¼	40	Thin upland, rolling, well timbered; branch water, oak timber; 4 miles of railroad.
S. fr. ½ & N.W. ¼ of S.E. ¼	112 21	
S.W. ¼	160 40	
Section 34.		
W. ½ & S.E. ¼ of N.W. ¼	120	Upland and bottom, well timbered; branch water; 6 miles from railroad.
S. ½ of S.E. ¼	80	
E. ½ & N.W. ¼ of S.W. ¼	120	
Section 36.		
N.E. ¼	160	Rolling upland, well timbered; black, white and post oak; N.E. ¼ well improved; eight miles of railroad.
W. ½ & N.E. ¼ of N.W. ¼	120	
W. ½ of S.E. ¼	80	
S.W. ¼	160	
42, *Range* 4 *East.*		
Section 2.		
S.W. ¼ of N.E. ¼	40	Rolling upland, well timbered with oak; branch water.
Lot 2 & W. ½ of lot 1 N.W. ¼	136 28	
S.E. ¼	160	
W. ½ & N. E. ¼ of S.W. ¼	120	
Section 4.		
N.E. fr. ¼	56 39	Same.
N. ½ & S.W. ¼ of S.E. ¼	114 52	
E. ½ of S.W. ¼	80	
Section 6.		
Lot 1 N.E. ¼	80	Same.
S.E. ¼	160	
Section 8.		
N.W. ¼	160	Same.
E. ½ of section	320	
Section 10.		
E. ½ of N.W. ¼	80	Upland and bottom, well timbered and watered; varieties of oak.
S.E. ¼	160	
E. ½ & N.W. ¼ of S.W. ¼	120	
Section 12	640	Rolling upland, well timbered; spring and branch water.
Section 14.		
S.E. ¼	160	Same.
W. ½ & S.E. ¼ of S.E. ¼	120	
W. ½ of section	320	
Section 18.		
N.E. ¼	160	Same.
N.E. ¼ of S.E. ¼	40	
Lot 1 N.W. ¼	80	
Section 20.		
N.E. ¼	160	Same.
S. ½ of N.W. ¼	80	
S. ½ of section	320	
Section 22.		
W. ½ of N.W. ¼	80	Same.
N.E. ¼	160	
S. ½ of section	320	

TOWNSHIP.	Area. Acres 100ths.	DESCRIPTIVE NOTES.
Section 24.		
N.E. ¼ & S.W. ¼ of N.E. ¼	80	Upland and bottom, well timbered; varieties of oak; spring and branch water.
N.W. ¼ of S.E. ¼	40	
W. ½ of section	320	
Section 26	640	Rolling upland, well timbered; varieties of oak.
Section 28.		
N.E. ¼ & S.W. ¼ of S.E. ¼	80	Same.
S.E. ¼ of S.W. ¼	40	
N. ½ of section	320	
Section 30.		
E. ½ of N.E. ¼	80	Upland and bottom; black, white and post oak; branch water.
Lot 2 & S. ½ of lot 1 N.W. ¼	144 40	
N. ½ of lot 2 S.W. ¼	53	
Section 32.		
W. ½ of N.E. ¼	80	Gently rolling upland; oak timber and branch water.
N.W. ¼	160	
N. ½ of S.E. ¼	80	
N. ½ of S.W. ¼	80	
Section 34.		
E. ½ & N.W. ¼ of N.E. ¼	120	Thin upland, broken, well timbered, with varieties of oak.
N.E. ¼ of N.W. ¼	40	
N.E. ¼ of S.E. ¼	40	
S.W. ¼ of S.W. ¼	40	
Section 36.		
E. ½ of N.E. ¼	80	Same.
W. ½ & N.E. ¼ of N.W. ¼	120	
S.E. ¼	160	
W. ½ & S.E. ¼ of S.W. ¼	120	
41, *Range* 4 *East*.		
Section 2.		
N. ½ of section	412 96	Same.
N. ½ of S.E. ¼	80	
S.E. ¼ of S.W. ¼	40	
Section 4.		
W. ½ lot 1 of N.E. ¼	40	Rolling upland, well timbered; white, black and post oak; spring and branch water.
Lot 1 N.W. ¼	80	
W. ½ & N.E. ¼ of S.E. ¼	120	
S.E. ¼ of S.W. ¼	40	
Section 6.		
Lot 1 N.E. ¼	80	Hilly and broken, well timbered; oaks.
S.E. fr. ¼	157 83	
S.W. fr. ¼	72 45	
Section 8.		
N.E. ¼	160	Same.
N.E. ¼ of S.E. ¼	40	
S.W. ¼ of S.W. ¼	40	
W. ½ & S.E. ¼ of S.W. ¼	120	
Section 10.		
W. ½ of S.W. ¼	83	Ridge land, well timbered, with white and post oak.

TOWNSHIP.	Area. Acres	100ths.	DESCRIPTIVE NOTES.
Section 18.			
N.E. fr. ¼	55	88	Rolling upland; varieties of oak; soil thin.
S. fr. ¼ of section	318	16	
Section 20.			
W. ½ of section	320		Same.
S.W. ¼ of N.E. ¼	40		
W. ½ of S.E. ¼	80		
Section 30	687	64	Same.
43, *Range* 8 *East*.			
Section 22.			
S.E. fr. ¼	22		Broken upland; 2 acres in cultivation.
Section 24	588	55	Broken upland, timbered with oak and hickory; 3½ miles from railroad.
Section 26	634	25	Same.
Section 28.			
E. ½ of section	302	86	Same.
S.W. ¼	160		
W. ½ & S.E. ¼ of N.W. ¼	120		
Section 30.			
N.E. ¼ of S.E. ¼	40		Same.
Section 32.			
E. ½ of N.E. ¼	80		Same.
Section 36.			
S.E. fr. ¼	150	45	Same; 4 miles from railroad.
N. ½ of section	317	95	
N. ½ of S.W. ¼	80		
42, *Range* 8 *East*.			
Section 2.			
N. ½ of section	262	64	Broken upland, timbered; oak and hickory.
N. ½ of S.E. ¼	79		
W. ½ & N.E. ¼ of S.W. ¼	120		
Section 4.			
W. ½ of lot 1 of N.E. ¼	39	35	Same, with stock water.
S.E. ¼	160		
Section 6.			
E. ½ of section	286	50	Broken upland, fine oak timber; bed of iron ore; 3 miles from railroad.
S. ½ of N.W. ¼	53	33	
Lot 1 S.W. ¼	80		
Section 8.			
S.E. ¼	160		Ridge land, good soil; white oak and hickory; 4 miles from railroad.
E. ½ of S.W. ¼	80		
Section 10.			
W. ½ of N.E. ¼	80		Broken and ridge land; white and post oak, with improvement on N.W. ¼; well watered. 6 miles from railroad.
N.W. ¼	160		
W. ½ & N.E. ¼ of S.W. ¼	120		
Section 14.			
W. ½ of N.W. ¼	80		Ridge land, heavy timber; white and post oak.

TOWNSHIP.	Area. Acres	100ths.	DESCRIPTIVE NOTES.
Section 18.			
S.W. ¼ of N.E. ¼	40		Ridge, heavy timber; white, black and red oak and hickory; 5 miles from railroad.
S. ½ lot 1 of N.W. ¼	40	59	
Lot 2 S.W. ¼	46	10	
Section 20.			
N. ½ of N.E. ¼	80		Ridge land, well timbered with oak and hickory; watered; three improvements on section; 5 miles from railroad.
N.W. ¼	160		
S.E. ¼ of S.E. ¼	40		
E. ½ & N.W. ¼ of S.W. ¼	120		
Section 22.			
W. ½ & S.E. ¼ of N.E. ¼	120		Ridge land, well timbered; oak and hickory; just outside of 6 miles limit.
N.W. ¼ of S.E. ¼	40		
W. ½ & N.E. ¼ of S.W. ¼	120		
Section 24.			
S.E. ¼ of S.E. ¼	40		Same.
Section 26.			
N.W. fr. ¼	101	98	Same.
S.E. ¼ of S.W. ¼	40		
Section 28.			
S.W. ¼ of N.E. ¼	40		Ridge land, oak and hickory; improved; outside of 6 miles limit.
N. ½ of N.W. ¼	80		
Section 30.			
Lot 2 & S. ½ of lot 1 of N.W. ¼	94	90	Ridge land, heavy timber, well watered; 5 miles from railroad.
N. ½ of lot 1 of S.W. ¼	88	81	
W. ½ & S.E. ¼ of S.E. ¼	120		
Section 32.			
E. ½ & N.W. ¼ of N.W. ¼	120		Same.
S. ½ of N.E. ¼	80		
S.W. ¼ of S.W. ¼	40		
Section 34.			
W. ½ & S.E. ¼ of N.E. ¼	120		Ridge land, oak and kickory; branch water; 3 improvements on the section; outside of 6 miles limit.
E. ½ & N.W. ¼ of N.W. ¼	120		
S. ½ & N.E. ¼ of S.E. ¼	120		
S.E. ¼ of S.W. ¼	40		
N.W. ¼ of S.W. ¼	40		
Section 36.			
[illegible]. ½ of section	131	19	Same; improvement on tract.
41, *Range* 8 *East.*			
Section 2.			
E. ½ of section	310	44	Same; improvement on N.W. ¼.
N.W. ¼	158	2	
E. ½ & S.W. ¼ of S.W. ¼	120		
Section 4.			
Lot 2 & W. ½ of lot 1 N.E. ¼	131	28	Ridge land, well timbered; oak and hickory, with water; improvement on N.W. ¼.
Lot 1 & E. ½ of lot 2 N.W. ¼	125	10	
S. ½ of S.E. ¼	80		
N.E. ¼ of S.W. ¼	40		

TOWNSHIP.	Area. Acres 100ths.	DESCRIPTIVE NOTES.
Section 6.		
N.E. ¼ & S.W. ¼ of S.E. ¼	80	Same.
S.W. ¼	154	
Section 8.		
N. ½ of section	320	Gently rolling and ridge upland, well timbered; oak and hickory; improvement on S.E. ¼.
N. ½ of S.E. ¼	80	
N. ½ of S.W. ¼	80	
Section 10.		
E. ½ & S.W. ¼ of N.E. ¼	120	Ridge land, well timbered; oak and hickory; spring water; improvement; house and farm on N.W. ¼; 2 miles from Morse's mill.
W. ½ & S.E. ¼ of N. W. ¼	120	
N. ½ of S.W. ¼	80	
Section 14.		
N. fr. ½ of section	185	Ridge land, well timbered; oak and hickory; 1 mile from Morse's mill.
Section 18.		
W. ½ of N.E. ¼	80	Same.
S.E. ¼	160	
Lot 1 & W. ½ lot 2 of N.W. ¼	116 89	
N. ½ of lots 1 & 2 of S.W. ¼	79	
Section 20.		
E. ½ of section	320	Gently rolling and bottom land, well timbered; oak and hickory; improvements on N.W. & N.E. ¼; spring water.
W. ½ & S.E. ¼ of N. W. ¼	120	
E. ½ & N.W. ¼ of S. W. ¼	120	
Section 22, fr	16	Timbered land.
Section 24.		
E. ½ of N.E. ¼	80	Ridge land; white and post oak timber river water.
S. fr. ½ of section	184 72	
Section 28.		
N.E. fr. ¼	50 94	Bluff and bottom land, well timbered, with plenty of water; improvement on N.E. ¼.
E. ½ & N.W. ¼ of N. W. ¼	120	
E. ½ of S.W. ¼	80	
Section 30.		
S.E. ¼ of N.E. ¼	40	Ridge land; white, black and post oak; part bottom; rich land, well watered.
E. ½ of S.E. ¼	80	
Lot 1 & S. ½ of lot 2 N.W. ¼	120 42	
Lot 2 of S.W. ¼	85 12	
Section 32.		
N. E. fr. ¼	66 36	Ridge land, oak timber.
Section 34 fr.	72 58	Big river bottom.
Section 36.		
N. ½ of section	320	Gently sloping ridge, fine timber; oak and hickory; spring water; N.E. ¼ improved.
E. ½ & N.W. ¼ of S.W. ¼	120	
40, *Range* 3 *East*.		
Section 2.		
E. ½ of lot 2 of N.E. ¼	57 36	Ridge land, thin oak and hickory.
W. ½ of lots 1 & 2 of N.W. ¼	100 26	
N.W. ¼ of S.W. ¼	40	

TOWNSHIP.	Area. Acres 100ths.	DESCRIPTIVE NOTES.
Section 4.		
E. fr. ½ of section	73 10	Broken upland, timbered; oak and hickory; spring water.
W. ½ of N.W. ¼	145 03	
Section 6 fr.	535 25	Upland, oak and hickory; spring water; on S.W. ¼ improvements.
Section 8.		
S. fr. ½	238 93	Rolling ridge land, well timbered; oak and hickory; river water.
S.W. ¼ of N.W. ¼	40	
Section 18.		
N. ½ of section	314 48	Same.
N.E. ¼ of S.E. ¼	40	
42, Range 2 East.		
Section 24.		
N.E. ¼ of N.E. ¼	40	Rolling ridge land, oak timber, fair soil.
S.W. ¼ of S.E. ¼	40	
Section 36.		
N.W. ¼ of N.W. ¼	40	Same.
W. ½ of S.E. ¼	80	
E. ½ & S.W. ¼ of S.W. ¼	120	
41, Range 2 East.		
Section 2.		
E. ½ of N.E. ¼ & S.E. ¼	198 26	High rolling upland, good timber, oak; branch water.
Section 12.		
E. ½ of section	320	Same.
S. ½ of S.W. ¼	80	
E. ½ & N.W. ¼ of N.W. ¼ ...	120	
Section 14.		
E. ½ & N.W. ¼ of N.E. ¼ ...	126 66	Same.
Section 24.		
N.W. ¼	160	Same.
S. ½ of N.E. ¼	80	
E. ½ of S.E. ¼	80	
E. ½ & S.W. ¼ of S.W. ¼ ...	120	
Section 26.		
N. ½ of section	486 48	Gently rolling upland, well timbered with white and black oak; branch water.
S.E. ¼	166 72	
E. ½ of S.W. ¼	83 36	
Section 36.		
W. ½ of N.W. ¼	80	Broken upland, timbered with oak; branch water.
N.W. ¼ of S.W. ¼	40	
40, Range 2 East.		
Section 2.		
Lot 2 & E. ½ of lot 1 N.E. ¼	120	Gently rolling upland, thin soil, good oak timber; branch water.
Lots 1 & 2 of N.W. ¼	159 40	
W. ½ of S.W. ¼	80	

TOWNSHIP.	Area. Acres 100ths.	DESCRIPTIVE NOTES.
Section 12.		
N. ½ of N.E. ¼	81 20	High rolling upland, well timbered with oak; spring and branch water.
E. ½ & N.W. ¼ of N.W. ¼	120	
N. ½ & S.W. ¼ of S.E. ¼	112 72	
E. ½ & S.W. ¼ of S.W. ¼	120	
Section 14 fr	74 06	Timber land.
Section 24.		
N.W. fr. ¼	82 77	Same.

WASHINGTON COUNTY.

35,410 $\frac{88}{100}$ ACRES.

Sale commences ***TUESDAY****, October* **11*th***, 1859.

TOWNSHIP.	Area. Acres 100ths.	DESCRIPTIVE NOTES.
40, *Range 2 East.*		
Section 18.		
S. ½ of section	334 72	Gently rolling upland, well timbered; white, black and post oak.
Section 20.		
W. ½ of section	320	
E. fr. ½ of N.E. ¼	72 40	Good upland; spring; well timbered; varieties of oak.
Section 30.		
N.W. ¼	168 60	Upland, broken, timbered with red oak; in mineral range.
E. ½ of N.E. ¼	80	
N.E. ¼ of S.W. ¼	40	
39, *Range 2 East.*		
Section 6.		
Lots 2 & 3 & W. ½ lot 1 NE. ¼	167 36	Broken and hilly, timbered; 1 mile from Rich Woods; mineral land.
S.W. fr. ¼	75 24	
40, *Range 1 East.*		
Section 18.		
S.E. ¼	160	Broken and hilly, timbered; pin oak; in mineral range.
Section 20.		
E. ½ of section	320	Broken and thin upland, some young pine; in mineral range.
S.W. ¼	160	
Section 22.		
N. ½ of section	348 48	Broken upland, timbered with white and black oak; branch and spring water; in mineral range.
S.E. ¼	170 12	
W. ½ & N.E. ¼ of S.W. ¼	127 59	

TOWNSHIP.	Area. Acres 100ths.	DESCRIPTIVE NOTES.
Section 24.		
E. ½ of section	320	Hilly upland, timbered with white and black oak; branch water; E. ½ of S.W. ¼ improved; in mineral range.
E. ½ of N.W. ¼	80	
E. ½ of S.W. ¼	80	
Section 26.		
S. ½ of section	335 76	Broken upland, timbered; mineral land; old diggings.
W. ½ of N.W. ¼	83 84	
E. ½ of N.E. ¼	83 84	
Section 28.		
E. ½ & N.W. ¼ of N.E. ¼	124 62	Pine lands, on range of Gilmore load—fine lead land.
E. ½ & N.W. ¼ of N.W. ¼	124 62	
S.W. ¼	166 56	
N.E. ¼ & S.W. ¼ of S.E. ¼	83 28	
Section 30.		
E. ½ & N. W. ¼ of N.E. ¼	120	2d rate upland, pine lands.
E. ½ & N.W. ¼ of S.E. ¼	120	
Lot 2 & S. ½ of lot 1 N.W. ¼	116 89	
S.W. ¼	170 25	
Section 32.		
N.E. ¼	160	Good upland, well watered and timbered; oak and pine.
E. ½ of S.E. ¼	80	
E. ½ & N.W. ¼ of N.W. ¼	120	
S.W. ¼	160	
Section 34	657 60	Upland, watered and well timbered; oak and pine; range of Gilmore load; fine lead land.
Section 36.		
W. ½ of section	320	Upland, watered and timbered; varieties of oak; Cabanné diggings; fine lead lands.
W. ½ of S.E. ¼	80	
39, *Range* 1 *East*.		
Section 2.	772 24	Pine lands, 2d rate; arable spring and branch water.
Section 4.		
E. ½ of section	392 34	First rate pine lands, improvement; gently rolling; well watered; Bauhn steam mill on section.
S.W. ¼	160	
Lots 1, 2 & W. ½ of lot 3 NW¼	187 51	
Section 6	726 20	Broken upland, heavy timbered, varieties of oak; spring water; fine mineral indications.
Section 8	640	2nd rate upland, pine and oak timber, spring and branch water.
Section 10.		
E. ½ of section	320	Gently rolling upland, pine, white and black oak timber, spring and branch water; S.W. ¼ improved.
S.W. ¼	160	
E. ½ & S.W. ¼ of N.W. ¼	120	
Section 12.		
N. ½ of section	320	Pine lands, spring and branch water.
N. ½ of S.W. ¼	80	
Section 14.		
N. ½ of N.E. ¼	80	Pine lands.
N.W. ¼	160	

TOWNSHIP.	Area. Acres	100ths.	DESCRIPTIVE NOTES.
Section 18.			
E. ½ & S.W. ¼ of N.E. ¼	120		Thin upland, post and black oak timber; branch water.
W. ½ & S.E. ¼ of S.E. ¼	120		
S. ½ of lot 1 & N. ½ lot 2 N.W. ¼	72	5	
S. ½ of lot 1 & N. ½ of lot 2 of S.W. ¼	75	83	
Section 20.			
W. ½ & S.E. ¼ of N.E. ¼ ...	120		2nd rate upland, varieties of oak timber; branch water.
W. ½ & S.E. ¼ of N.W. ¼ ...	120		
S. ½ of section	320		
Section 22.			
W. ½ & N.E. ¼ of N.W. ¼ ..	120		Gently rolling upland; white, black and post oak; branch water.
Section 28.			
W. ½ & N.E. ¼ of N.W. ¼ ..	120		Same.
Section 30	614	84	Thin upland, well timbered, varieties of oak; branch water; mineral region.
Section 32.			
W. ½ & N.E. ¼ of N.W. ¼ ..	120		Same.
38, *Range* 1 *East.*			
Section 6.			
W. ½ of N.W. ¼	87	95	Rough upland, pine and oak, mineral land.
40, *Range* 1 *West.*			
Section 14.			
S. ½ of section	320		Broken upland, oak and hickory; water; mineral land; mineral range.
Section 18.			
E. ½ & S.W. ¼ of S.E. ¼ ...	120		Mineral section, Murphy's diggings and other diggings; valuable for mineral (lead).
S. ½ of S.W. ¼	85	93	
Section 20.			
N. ½ of section	320		2d rate upland, well timbered and watered, varieties of oak; in mineral range.
S.E. ¼	160		
W. ½ & N.E. ¼ of S.W. ¼ ..	120		
Section 22.			
W. ½ of section	320		Thin upland, black and white oak timber; mineral range and mineral sign (lead).
S.E. ¼	160		
W. ½ & N.E. ¼ of N.E. ¼ ..	120		
Section 24.			
E. ½ of N. E. ¼	83	38	Broken upland, arable, oak and sugar tree; well watered; mineral range.
W. ½ of N.W. ¼	83	38	
W. ½ of S.E. ¼	83	12	
.W. ½	166	24	
Section 26	640		Broken upland, well timbered, stock water; varieties of oak; small improvement on E. ½ of S.E. ¼; mineral range.
Section 28	640		Broken upland, timbered; varieties of oak; in mineral range.
Section 30.			
N.E. ¼	160		Gently rolling, well watered and timbered; varieties of oak; in mineral range; improvement on N. ½ of S.E. ¼.
E. ½ & N.W. ¼ of S.E. ¼	120		
S. ½ of lot 1 & N. ½ lot 2 N E. ¼	83	45	
S.E. ¼ of S.W. ¼	40		

TOWNSHIP.	Area. Acres 100ths.	DESCRIPTIVE NOTES.
Section 32.		
E. ½ & N.W. ¼ of N.W. ¼	120	Broken upland, white, black and post oak timber; in mineral range.
N.E. ¼	160	
N. ½ of S.E. ¼	80	
E. ½ of S.W. ¼	80	
Section 34	640	Same.
Section 36.		
E. ½ of N.W. ¼	82 43	Same.
E. ½ of section	326 48	
S.W. ¼	161 62	
89, *Range* 1 *West.*		
Section 2.		
N. ½ & S.E. ¼ of section	814 46	Upland and bottom, good soil, well timbered and watered, oak and hickory; improvement on N.W. ¼; in mineral range.
E. ½ & N.W. ¼ of S.W. ¼	120	
Section 4	1149 06	Thin upland, varieties of oak; in mineral range.
Section 6.		
Lots 1, 5 & 6 & E. ½ of lots 2, 3 & 4 of N.E. ¼	291 20	Broken upland, lead lands, old diggings; Hill's furnace on section; N.E. ¼ improv'd.
Lots 5 & 6 E. ½ of lot 4 & W. ½ of lot 2 of N.W. ¼	278 42	
W. ½ of S.E. ¼	80	
Section 8.		
S.E. ¼ of N.E. ¼	40	Broken, post oak land, in mineral range; Green's lead mines on N.W. ¼.
S.E. ¼	160	
S. ½ of S.W. ¼	80	
Section 10	640	Broken and hilly, varieties of oak; in mineral range.
Section 12.		
W. ½ of section	339 94	Same.
W. ½ of N.E. ¼	84 98	
S.E. ¼	169 48	
Section 14	640	Thin upland, varieties of oak, stock water, N.W. ¼ improved; in mineral range.
Section 18.		
N. ½ of section	349 60	Thin upland, varieties of oak timber, spring water; improvement on S.E. ¼ of S.E. ¼; all in mineral range.
W. ½ of S.W. ¼	105 30	
S.E. ¼ of S.E. ¼	40	
Section 20	640	Ridge land, varieties of oak timber, spring water, S.W. ¼ of S.W. ¼ improved; all in mineral range.
Section 22.		
N. ½ of section	320	Upland and bottom, 2d rate farming; oak and hickory; branch water; in min'l range.
S.W. ¼	160	
W. ½ & N.E. ¼ of S.E. ¼	120	
Section 24.		
N. ½ of section	320	Same as above; N.E. & N.W. ¼ improved.
S.E. ¼	160	
E. ½ & S.W. ¼ of S.W. ¼	120	

TOWNSHIP.	Area. Acres 100ths.	DESCRIPTIVE NOTES.
Section 26.		
E. ½ of N.W. ¼	80	2d rate upland, pine and oak, stock water; in mineral range.
E.E. ¼	160	
N. ½ & N.W. ¼ of S.E. ¼	120	
E. ½ & S.W. ¼ of S.W. ¼	120	
Section 28	640	Same.
Section 30.		
E. ½ of section	320	2nd rate upland, hill and bottom; hickory and oak timber; N.W. ¼ improved; all in mineral range.
Lot 1 S.W. ¼	80	
Lot 2 & S.½ lot 1 of N.W.¼	141 32	
Section 32	640	Pine land; Grant's saw mill on S. ½ of N.W. ¼; in mineral range.
Section 34	640	Fair upland; pine, oak and hickory; well watered; N.E. ¼ improved; Smith's saw mill on S.W. ¼.
Section 36.		
N. ½ of section	320	Broken upland; pine and oak timber; water; mineral land with lead diggings on it.
S.E. ¼	160	
N.E.¼ & S.W.¼ of S.W.¼	80	
38, *Range* 1 *West.*		
Section 2.		
Lots 2 & 3 of N.E.¼	145 49	Pine lands; lead lands; lead is now raised on section.
W. ½ of section	361 24	
Section 4	707 50	Pine lands; also mineral, close to Grant's steam mill.
Section 6.		
N.E. ¼	161 28	Rolling upland; also bottom; timber—oak, hickory, sugartree and walnut; spring and creek water; S.E. ¼ improved lead lands.
S. ½ of section	332 60	
W. ½ of lot 1 of N.W. ¼	42 89	
Section 8.		
N. ½ of section	320	Broken upland; pine and oak timber; lead land.
S.E. ¼	160	
W. ½ & S.E. ¼ of S.W. ¼	120	
Section 10	640	Pine lands; in mineral range; timbered heavy.
Section 12.		
N. ½ of N.W. ¼	80	Same.
Section 18	671 48	Upland, part rolling; timber—oak and elm; well watered; in mineral range.
Section 20	640	Same; S.W. ¼ improved.
Section 30	653 38	Broken upland; varieties of oak; mineral land.
40, *Range* 2 *West.*		
Section 24.		
W. ½ & N.E. ¼ of N.E. ¼	120	Broken and hilly; lead land.
Section 36.		
E. ½ of section	320	Upland; best quality lead lands.

TOWNSHIP.	Area. Acres 100ths.	DESCRIPTIVE NOTES.
39, *Range* 2 *West.*		
Section 12.		
E. ½ of section	320	Broken upland; well timbered with oak; lead land.
Section 24.		
E. ½ & N.W. ¼ of N.E. ¼	120	Thin upland; oak timber; well watered; mineral land.
W. ½ of S.E. ¼	80	
Section 36.		
E. ½ of N.E. ¼	80	Same.
S.E. ¼	160	
38, *Range* 2 *West.*		
Section 12.		
E. ½ of section	320	Broken upland; well timbered; oak and hickory; mineral range.
Section 24.		
E. ½ of section	320	Same; mineral section.
Section 36.		
W. ½ of N.E. ¼	80	Broken upland; mineral section.

FRANKLIN COUNTY.

84,241 $\frac{47}{100}$ Acres.

Sale commences MONDAY, October 17, 1859.

TOWNSHIPS.	Area. Acres 100ths.	DESCRIPTIVE NOTES.
45, *Range* 2 *East.*		
Section 26 fr.	23 10	High rolling upland; white and black oak timber.
Section 36.		
E. ½ and S.W. ¼ of N.W. ¼	120	Same.
E. ½ and N.W. ¼ of S.E. ¼	120	
S.W. ¼ of S.W. ¼	40	
44, *Range* 2 *East.*		
Section 12.		
W. ½ of S.E. ¼	84 18	Broken upland; white, and black oak timber; near Missouri river.
S.E. ¼ of S.W. ¼	42 9	
Section 14.		
E. ½ of N.E ¼	80	Same; 4 miles of railroad.
S.E. ¼	160	
S.E. ¼ & N.W. ¼ of S.W. ¼	80	

TOWNSHIP.	Area. Acres 100ths.	DESCRIPTIVE NOTES.
Section 22.		
W. ½ of S.W. ¼	80	Same.
S.E. ¼ of S.E. ¼	40	
N.E. ¼ of N.E. ¼	40	
Section 24.		
S.E ¼ of S.E. ¼	41 17	Same.
S.W. ¼ of S.W. ¼	41 17	
Section 26.		
N.W. ¼ of N.E. ¼	40	Same; 2½ miles of depot.
W. ½ & N.E. ¼ of N.W. ¼	120	
S.W. ¼ of S.E. ¼	40	
E. ½ of S.W. ¼	80	
Section 28.		
S. ½ of N.E. ¼	80	Rolling upland; fine timber—white and black oak; arable; branch water; 1½ miles from Gray's summit, Pacific railroad.
E. ½ of S.E. ¼	80	
S.W. ¼	160	
S.E. ¼ of N.W. ¼	40	
Section 32.		
E. ½ of N.E. ¼	80	Same; 1 mile from depot at Gray's summit.
Section 36.		
N.W. ¼ of N.W. ¼	40	Same; 3 miles of railroad.
43, *Range* 2 *East.*		
Section 4.		
N.W. ¼ of N.E. ¼	41 77	Broken upland; timbered—white and black oak; 1 mile from depot, Gray's summit.
N. ½ of N.W. ¼	93 51	
Section 32.		
N.E. ¼ of S.E. ¼	40	Gently rolling upland; black and white oak timber; ¾ mile from Calvé station.
42, *Range* 2 *East.*		
Section 4.		
N.W. ¼ of S.E. ¼	41 15	High rolling upland; white and black oak timber; ½ mile from Calvé station.
N.E. ¼ of S.W. ¼	40 95	
Section 6, fr.	137 22	Bluff of Meramec, 1 mile from Calvé station.
Section 8.		
E. ½ & N.W. ¼ of N.E. ¼	123 48	High rolling upland; timbered with white and black oak; 1 mile from Calvé station.
N.E. ¼ of N.W. ¼	40 16	
Section 10.		
E. ½ & N.W. ¼ of N.E. ¼	125 4	Same; 1½ miles from Calvé station.
W. ½ of N.W. ¼	83 36	
W. ½ of S.W. ¼	83 12	
Section 12.		
N.W. ¼ of N.E. ¼	40 61	High rolling upland; heavy timber—white, black and post oak; 2½ miles from Calvé station; two improvements on section; also Catholic church.
N.E. ¼ of N.W. ¼	41 59	
W. ½ & S.E. ¼ of S.E. ¼	124 58	
W. ½ & N.E. ¼ of S.W. ¼	124 59	

TOWNSHIP.	Area Acres	100ths.	DESCRIPTIVE NOTES.
Section 14.			
W. ½ of N.E. ¼	84	4	Same; improvement on tract 2½ miles from station.
N.W. ¼ of S.E. ¼	41	7	
W. ½ of S.W. ¼	84	14	
Section 22.			
S.W. ¼ of N.W. ¼	41	22	Same quality of land; 8 miles from station.
S.W. ¼	164	68	
Section 24.			
W. ½ of S.W. ¼	82	40	High rolling upland; white, black and post oak timber; 4½ miles from depot.
Section 26.			
S. ½ & N.E. ¼ of Section	502	4	High rolling upland; arable; heavy timber; white, black and post oak; 4 miles from depot.
W. ½ of N.W. ¼	88	86	
Section 28.			
N.E. ¼ of N.E. ¼	41	75	Thin upland; branch water; 5 miles from depot.
S.E. ¼ of S.E. ¼	41	75	
W. ½ of S.W. ¼	83	50	
Section 34.			
S.E. ¼ of N.E. ¼	40		Gently rolling upland; heavy timber—white, black and post oak; 6 miles from depot.
W. ½ & S.E. ¼ of S.E. ¼	120		
E. ½ & S.W. ¼ of S.W. ¼	120		
41, *Range* 2 *East*.			
Section 2.			
S. ½ of S.W. ¼	82	58	High rolling upland; oak timber; branch water.
Section 4.			
N.E. ¼ of N.E. ¼	58	37	Same.
S.E. ¼ of S.E. ¼	40		
Section 6.			
E. ½ & S.W. ¼ of S.E. ¼	120		Gently rolling; well timbered; white, black and post oak; 6 miles from Calvé station.
S. ½ of Lot 2 of S.W. ¼	84	73	
Section 10.			
N. ½ of N.E. ¼	85	32	same quality, outside of six miles limit.
W. ½ & N.E. ¼ of N.W. ¼	127	98	
Section 14.			
S.W. ¼ of N.W. ¼	42	22	Same.
Section 18.			
N.W. ¼ of N.E. ¼	40		Upland and bottom; oak timber; branch water.
N.E. ¼ of N.W. ¼	37	69	
W. ½ & S.E. ¼ of S.E. ¼	120		
E. ½ of S.W. ¼	79	12	
Section 20.			
N.W. ¼ of N.W. ¼	40		Gently rolling upland, timbered with oak.
Section 22.			
S. ½ of N.E. ¼	85	18	Gently rolling upland; spring and branch water; oak timber; improvement on it.
E. ½ of S.E. ¼	83	96	
S. ½ of N.W. ¼	85	98	

TOWNSHIP.	Area. Acres 100ths.	DESCRIPTIVE NOTES.
Section 30.		
E. ½ of S.E. ¼	80	Same quality.
S. ½ of Lot 2 of N.W. ¼	41 53	
S. ½ of Lots 1 & 2 of S.W. ¼	126	
Section 32.		
N.W. ¼	160	Same quality; branch water.
S. ½ of N.E. ¼	80	
S. ½ of S.E. ¼	80	
N.W. ¼ & S.E. ¼ of S.W. ¼	80	
Section 34.		
S. ½ of Section	320	Part broken, part gently rolling; timber oak; spring and branch water; part of it improved.
N.W. ¼	160	
S.E. ¼ of N.E. ¼	40	
40, *Range* 2 *East.*		
Section 4.		
W. ½ of Section	373 18	Gently rolling; heavy timber—white, black and post oak; spring and branch water; N.E. ¼ improved.
S. E. ¼	168 72	
E. ½ & S.W. ¼ of N.E. ¼	168 64	
Section 6.		
E. ½ of N.E. ¼	96 99	Gently rolling good upland; oak timber; branch water.
S.E. ¼	160	
E. ½ & N.W. ¼ of S.W. ¼	132 75	
W. ½ of Lots 1 & 2 of N.W. ¼	94 70	
Section 8.	640	Gently rolling good upland; heavy timber—white, black and post oak.
Section 10.		
N.W. ¼	167 12	Gently rolling thin upland; oak timber.
Section 18.		
N. ½ of Section	335 18	Gently rolling upland; good timber—white, black and post oak; improvement of north east quarter.
43, *Range* 1 *East.*		
Section 18.		
S.E. ¼ of S.E. ¼	40	Thin upland.
Section 20.		
S.E. ¼ of S.W. ¼	40	Same.
42, *Range* 1 *East.*		
Section 4.		
N.E. ¼ of N.E. ¼	31 11	High rolling second rate upland; oak and hickory timber; branch water; 1½ miles from depot.
N.W. ¼ of N.W. ¼	38 38	
Section 22.		
S.E. ¼ of S.E. ¼	39 37	Thin upland; mineral land, in lead range.
Section 30.		
N.E. ¼ of N.E. ¼	40	Gently rolling good upland; black and white oak timber; 1 mile from St. Clair.
S. ½ of Lots 1 & 2 of S.W. ¼	87 59	
Section 34.		
N.E. ¼ of N.W. ¼	37 33	Gently rolling; oak timber; spring water; in lead range.
N.E. ¼ of S.E. ¼	40	

TOWNSHIP.	Area. Acres 100ths.	DESCRIPTIVE NOTES.
41, *Range* 1 *East.*		
Section 2.		
S. ½ of N.W. ¼	93 85	Rolling upland; white, black and post oak timber; branch water; 5 miles from depot; lead range.
E. ½ & N.W. ¼ of S.W. ¼	120	
E. ½ & N.W. ¼ of S.E. ¼	120	
Section 6.		
S.W. ¼ of N.E. ¼	40	High rolling upland; oak timber; 1¼ miles from St. Clair.
W. ½ of S.E. ¼	80	
S.E. ¼ of S.W. ¼	40	
Section 10.		
N. E. ¼	160	Broken upland; oak timber; in lead range; branch water.
Section 12.		
S.W. ¼ of S.E. ¼	40	Gently rolling upland; oak timber.
S.W. ¼ of S.W. ¼	40	
Section 14.		
N.E. ¼	160	High rolling upland; well timbered; varieties of oak; branch water.
E. ½ of S.E. ¼	80	
W. ½ of S.W. ¼	80	
Section 18.		
W. ½ & S.E. ¼ of N.E. ¼	120	Hilly and broken; in lead range.
Section 20.		
W. fr. ½ of N.W. ¼	27 58	Hill and bottom; well timbered; river water.
W. ½ of S.W. ¼	81 98	
Section 22.		
E. ½ of N.E. ¼	80	High rolling, second rate upland; timbered with post and black oak.
S.E. ¼	160	
S.E. ¼ of S.W. ¼	40	
Section 24.		
W. ½ of section	320	Same quality.
S.E. ¼	160	
W. ½ & S.E. ¼ of N.E. ¼	120	
Section 26.		
W. ½ of N.W. ¼	80	Same quality, with spring and branch water.
W. ½ & N.E. ¼ of S.W. ¼	120	
S.W. ¼ of S.E. ¼	40	
Section 28.		
E. ½ & S.W. ¼ of S.W. ¼	120	Same quality; range of Virginia mines; good lead land.
Section 30.		
N.E. ¼	160	Hilly and broken; fine lead land; Kinner's load running through it.
S.W. ¼	151 93	
W. ½ of S.E. ¼	80	
Section 32.		
W. ½ of N.W. ¼	80	Broken upland; lead land.
S.W. ¼ of N.E. ¼	40	
Section 34.	640	Broken upland; well timbered—oak; in mineral range; lead land.

TOWNSHIP.	Area Acres	100ths.	DESCRIPTIVE NOTES.
Section 36.			
S.W. ¼	160		Thin upland; white and black oak timber; spring and branch water.
W. ½ of N.E. ¼ of N.E. ¼	120		
40, Range 1 East.			
Section 2.			
Lots 1 & 2 of N.E. ¼	160		High broken upland; oak timber; branch and spring water.
S.E. ¼	160		
N.W. ¼	200	11	
E. ½ & N.W. ¼ of S.W. ¼	120		
Section 4.			
E. ½ of section	406	81	Hill and bottom; white, black and post oak; branch water; in mineral range; lead land.
N.W. ¼	287	10	
Section 6.			
E. ½ of lot 2 of N.W. ¼	67	89	Broken upland; lead land.
S.E. ¼	160		
Section 8.			
E. ½ of section	320		Rolling upland; oak timber; fine lead section.
N.W. ¼	160		
N. ½ of S.W. ¼	80		
Section 10.			
N.E. ¼ of N.W. ¼	48	28	Rolling upland; oak timber; branch and spring water.
N.E. ¼	178	12	
E. ½ of S.E. ¼	86	68	
W. ½ & S.E. ¼ of S.W. ¼	180	2	
Section 12.			
N. ½ of section	320		Broken upland; white, black and post oak timber; spring water.
S.W. ¼	160		
Section 14.			
N.W. ¼ of N.W. ¼	40		Same quality.
Section 18.			
E. ½ of N.E. ¼	80		Gently rolling, second rate upland; oak and hickory; branch water.
Lot 2 & S. ½ of lot 1 of N.W. ¼	105	88	
43, Range 1 West.			
Section 18.			
Lot 3 of N.W. ¼	51	61	Broken upland; post and black oak timber.
Lots 2 & 3 of S.W. ¼	128	44	
Section 24.			
N.W. ¼ of N.E. ¼	40		Glady upland; no timber; copper sign.
N.E. ¼ of S.W. ¼	40		
Section 30.			
S.W. ¼ of N.E. ¼	40		Rolling upland; scattering oak timber; improvement on part of it.
Lot 1 & S. ½ of lot 3 of N.W. ¼	102	71	
Lot 2 of S.W. ¼	80		
E. ½ of S.E. ¼	80		
Section 32.			
N.W. ¼ of N.E. ¼	40		Second rate upland; timber—hickory and oak; spring and branch water.
N.W. ¼ of S.E. ¼ of S.E. ¼	80		
N.W. ¼ of S.E. ¼ of N.W. ¼	80		

TOWNSHIP.	Area. Acres 100ths.	DESCRIPTIVE NOTES.
42, Range 1 *West.*		
Section 2.		
E. ½ of N.E. ¼	100 24	Rolling upland; timber—oak and hickory.
S.E. ¼	160	
Section 4.		
W. ½ of S.E. ¼	80	Broken upland; white, post and black oak timber.
Section 6.		
W. ½ of lot 2 of N.E. ¼	54 22	Broken and thin upland; oak and hickory.
N. ½ of lot 1 of S.W. ¼	40	
Section 10.		
E. ½ of S.W. ¼	80	Same.
Section 14.		
S.E. ¼ of N.W. ¼	40	Rolling upland; oak and hickory; water; second rate tillable land; 2 miles from St. Clair.
W. ½ of S.E. ¼	80	
Section 18.		
E. ½ of S.E. ¼	80	Thin upland; white and black oak; stock water; mineral land.
S. ½ of lots 1 & 2 of N.W. ¼	80	
Lot 3 of S.W. ¼	56 34	
Section 20.		
N. ½ of section	320	Upland and bottom; oak and hickory; well watered; good farming and mineral land.
E. ½ & N.W. ¼ of S.W. ¼	120	
Section 26.		
S.E. ¼ of S.E. ¼	40	Hilly and broken; black and post oak; ¼ of mile from St. Clair.
Section 28.		
N.E. ¼ of S.W. ¼	40	Gently rolling; good soil; oak timber; 2 miles from St. Clair.
42, Range 1 *West.*		
Section 30.		
S.E. ¼ of N.W. ¼	58 58	Broken upland; timber—hickory and oak; stock water.
W. ½ of S.W. ¼	109 16	
Section 36.		
N.E. ¼ of N.E. ¼	40	Hilly upland; black and post oak timber; 1 mile from road.
41, Range 1 *West.*		
Section 10.		
S.W. ¼ of N.W. ¼	40	Gently rolling ridge land; oak and hickory; 300 yards from railroad.
N.W. ¼ of S.W. ¼	40	
Section 12.		
S.W. ¼	167 88	Broken upland; oak and hickory; 2 miles from road.
W. ½ of S.E. ¼	88 68	
Section 14.		
S.W. ¼	166 96	Same quality, two miles from road.
Section 18.		
S. ½ of S.E. ¼	80	Rolling upland; black, white and post oak timber; road passes through this section.
S. ½ of lot 2 of N.W. ¼	72 90	
S. ½ of lot 1 of S.W. ¼	40	

TOWNSHIP.	Area. Acres	100ths.	DESCRIPTIVE NOTES.
Section 20.			
N.E. ¼	167	96	Rolling upland; oak and hickory; second rate farming land, ¼ mile from road.
E. ½ & N.W. ¼ of N.W. ¼	125	67	
Section 22.			
S.W. ¼ of N.W. ¼	40		Same quality, 2 miles from road.
S.E. ¼ of S.W. ¼	40		
W. ½ of S.E. ¼	80		
Section 24.			
S. ½ of N.W. ¼	80		Rolling upland; varieties of oak; spring and branch water; improvement on S.E. ¼; in lead region.
W. ½ of S.E. ¼	83		
S.W. ¼	166		
Section 26.			
N.E. ¼	160		Gently sloping ridge land; fine timber—oak and hickory; well watered; in lead region.
E. ½ of N.W. ¼	64	97	
E. ½ & N.W. ¼ of S.E. ¼	120		
Section 28.			
W. ½ of section	320		Broken upland; oak timber; fine lead land.
S.W. ¼ of N.E. ¼	40		
N.W. ¼ of S.E. ¼	40		
Section 30.			
N.E. ¼ & S.W. ¼ of S.E. ¼	80		Rolling upland; white, black and post oak timber; second rate agricultural land; stock water convenient.
N. ½ of lots 1 & 2 of S.W. ¼	80	70	
Section 32, fr.	377	20	Broken upland; best quality of lead lands, north and adjoining Thomas's mines.
Section 34.			
S. ½ of section	320		Upland; oak and hickory; well watered; improvement on N.W. ¼; fine mineral land.
W. ½ of N.E. ¼	78	60	
N.W. ¼	150	94	
Section 36	653	76	Broken upland; timbered oaks, in mineral region.
40, *Range* 1 *West.*			
Section 2	766	14	Ridge land; white and black oak timber; first quality of lead lands.
Section 4.			
N. ½ of section	446	14	Broken upland; well timbered with oak; best lead section of free lands; 800,000 lbs. lead raised in last 18 months; Herrington's mines on section.
S.W. ¼	160		
W. ½ & N.E. ¼ of S.E. ¼	120		
Section 6.			
S. ½ of N.W. ¼	126	19	Hill and bottom; timber—oak and hickory; well watered.
S. ½ & N.W. ¼ of N.E. ¼	93	27	
S. ½ of S.E. ¼	80		
E. fr. ½ of S.W. ¼	63	88	
Section 8.			
S.W. ¼ of N.W. ¼	40		Broken upland; first quality of mineral land.
E. ½ & S.W. ¼ of N.E. ¼	120		
S. ½ of section	320		
Section 10.			
S. ½ of section	320		Broken upland; timber—white and black oak; first quality of mineral land.
S. ½ of N.E. ¼	80		
W. ½ & S.E. ¼ of N.W. ¼	120		

TOWNSHIP.	Area Acres 100ths.	DESCRIPTIVE NOTES.
Section 12.		
N.E. ¼ of N.E. ¼	41 42	Broken upland; well timbered—varieties of oak; well watered.
S.E. ¼ of S.E. ¼	41 52	
E. ½ & S.W. ¼ of N.W. ¼	123 98	
W. ½ of S.W. ¼	88 5	
Section 14.		
N. ½ of section	320	Broken upland; well timbered—oak and hickory; stock water; mineral land.
Section 18.		
W. ½ & S.E. ¼ of N.E. ¼	120	Upland, well timbered—white, black and post oak; Murphy's digings on this land; first quality of lead land.
N.E. ¼ of N.W. ¼	40	
44, Range 2 West.		
Section 26.		
S.W. ¼ of N.E. ¼	40	Upland; timber—post and black oak.
Section 34.		
N.W. ¼ of N.W. ¼	40	Same.
43, Range 2 West.		
Section 2.		
W. ½ of N.W. ¼	87 27	Hilly and broken; black and white oak.
Section 12.		
S.E. ¼	160	Same quality.
N.W. ¼ of S.W. ¼	40	
Section 14.		
S.W. ¼ of N.E. ¼	40	Same quality.
E. ½ & N.W. ¼ of S.W. ¼	120	
Section 22.		
N.W. ¼ of N.W. ¼	40	Hill and bottom; oak and hickory timber; well watered by St. John's creek.
N.W. ¼ of S.W. ¼	40	
S.E. ¼ of N.E. ¼	40	
W. ½ of S.E. ¼	80	
Section 24.		
W. ½ & S.E. ¼ of N.W. ¼	120	Rolling upland, some bottom; black and post oak timber; spring and branch water.
S.W. ¼ of N.E. ¼	40	
W. ½ of S.E. ¼	80	
S.W. ¼	160	
Section 26.		
S.W. ¼ of N.W. ¼	40	Rolling upland; black and post oak timber; branch water.
N.W. ¼ of S.E. ¼	40	
S.W. ¼	160	
Section 28.		
N.E. ¼ of N.W. ¼	40	Pin oak glade.
S.W. ¼ of S.E. ¼	40	
S.E. ¼ of S.W. ¼	40	
Section 34.		
S. ½ of N.E. ¼	80	Broken upland; white and black oak timber; branch water.
E. ½ & S.W. ¼ of S.E. ¼	120	
N.E. ¼ of S.W. ¼	40	
W. ½ & N.E. ¼ of N.W. ¼	120	

TOWNSHIP.	Area. Acres	100ths.	DESCRIPTIVE NOTES.
Section 36.			
S.W. ¼ of S.W. ¼	40		Same.
42, *Range 2 West.*			
Section 2.			
N. ½ of N.E. ¼	77	85	Ridge land; post and black oak timber.
S.W. ¼ & N.E. ¼ of N.W. ¼	78	82	
S.W. ¼ of S.E. ¼	40		
W. ½ & S.E. ¼ of S.W. ¼	120		
Section 4.			
Lot 1 of N.E. ¼	80		Same.
W. ½ of lot 2 of N.W. ¼	32	80	
E. ½ & S.W. ¼ of S.E. ¼	120		
S. ½ of S.W. ¼	80		
Section 10.			
E. ½ & S.W. ¼ of N.E. ¼	120		Same.
W. fr. ½ of N.W. ¼	53		
N.W. ¼ of S.E. ¼	38	50	
Section 12.			
S. E. ¼ of N.E. ¼	40		Same.
N. ½ of S.W. ¼	80		
Section 14.			
N.E. ¼ of N.E. ¼	40		Broken upland; post oak and black oak.
S. ½ of S.W. ¼	80		
Section 22.			
E. fr. ½ of section	83	80	Same.
Section 24.			
E. ½ of N.E. ¼	80		Upland and bottom; bottom rich; timber—large and heavy, varieties of oak and hickory; well watered.
N.W. ¼ & S.E. ¼ of N.W. ¼	80		
S.E. ¼	160		
E. ½ of S.W. ¼	80		
Section 26.			
W. fr. ½ of section	278	95	Same.
N.E. ¼	160		
N.W. ¼ & S.E. ¼ of S.E. ¼	80		
Section 36.			
N.W. ¼	160		Same.
W. ½ & S.E. ¼ of N.E. ¼	120		
S.E. ¼	160		
E. ½ & N.W. ¼ of S.W. ¼	120		
41, *Range 2 West.*			
Section 2.			
Lots 2 & 3 of N.E. ¼	182	65	Broken upland; well timbered; varieties of oak; river water.
Lot 2 of N.W ¼	127	16	
S.E. ¼ of S.E. ¼	40		
Section 4.			
N. fr. ½ of S.E. ¼	80	50	Same quality of land.
S.W. fr. ¼	61	60	

TOWNSHIP.	Area. Acres	100ths.	DESCRIPTIVE NOTES.
Section 10.			
N.W. ¼ of N.E. ¼	40		Same.
Section 14.			
S.E. ¼ of N.W. ¼	40		Rolling ridge land; well timbered—oak.
Section 24.			
W. ½ of N.E. ¼	84	2	Ridge land; oak timber; one mile from depot.
E. ½ of N.W. ¼	84	2	
Section 28.			
N. ½ of section	320		Ridge land; well timbered; 1¼ miles from road.
S.W. ¼	160		
N.W. ¼ of S.E. ¼	40		
Section 34.			
S.E. ¼ of S.E. ¼	40		Same quality; on road.
W. ½ & S.E. ¼ of S.W. ¼	120		
Section 36.			
S.W. ¼ & N.E. ¼ of S.W. ¼	80		Same quality; ¾ mile of road.
40, *Range* 2 *West.*			
Section 2.			
E. ½ of lot 1 of N.W. ¼	40	47	White oak ridges; ½ mile from road.
S.E. ¼ & N.W. ¼ of S.W. ¼	80		
S. ½ of S.E. ¼	80		
Section 4.			
Lots 2 & 3 of N.E. ¼	150	62	Level ridge land; post and black oak timber; good farming land; ¾ mile from road.
Lot 3 of N.W. ¼	70	40	
N.E. ¼ of S.W. ¼	40		
Section 10.			
S.E. ¼	160		Rolling upland; white and black oak timber; well watered with branch water; ½ mile from road; mineral range.
S. ½ of S.W. ¼	80		
Section 12.			
W. ½ of section	327	86	White oak ridge land; watered by Bourbois River; mineral range.
S.E. ¼	182	59	
E. ½ & N.W. ¼ of N.E. ¼	124	14	
Section 14.			
N. ½ of section	320		Same quality.

CRAWFORD COUNTY.

13,328 $\frac{21}{100}$ Acres.

Sale commences FRIDAY, October 21, 1859.

TOWNSHIP.	Area. Acres	100ths.	DESCRIPTIVE NOTES.
40, *Range* 2 *West.*			
Section 14.			
N.E. ¼ & S.W. ¼ of S.E. ¼	80		Broken upland; white oak timber; in mineral region.
E. ½ of S.W. ¼	80		

TOWNSHIPS.	Area. Acres 100ths.	DESCRIPTIVE NOTES.

Section 22.

N.W. $\frac{1}{4}$.................. 160
W. $\frac{1}{2}$ of N.E. $\frac{1}{4}$............ 80 } Same; lead lands.
N.E. $\frac{1}{4}$ of S.W. $\frac{1}{4}$......... 40

Section 26.

E. $\frac{1}{4}$ & S.W. $\frac{1}{4}$ of N.E. $\frac{1}{4}$...109 28)
W. $\frac{1}{4}$ & N.E. $\frac{1}{4}$ of S.E. $\frac{1}{4}$...101 47 } Same; lead lands.
S. $\frac{1}{2}$ of N.W. $\frac{1}{4}$........... 80
N.W. $\frac{1}{4}$ of S.W. $\frac{1}{4}$......... 40

Section 28.

W. $\frac{1}{2}$ of N.W. $\frac{1}{4}$............ 80)
E. $\frac{1}{4}$ & S.W. $\frac{1}{4}$ of N.E. $\frac{1}{4}$...120 } Same; lead lands; rich diggings on section.
S. $\frac{1}{2}$ of section............ 320

Section 34.

N.W. $\frac{1}{4}$.................. 160 } Same; lead lands.
S.W. $\frac{1}{4}$ of N.E. $\frac{1}{4}$......... 40

Section 36.

E. $\frac{1}{4}$ & N.W. $\frac{1}{4}$ of N.W. $\frac{1}{4}$...120 } Same; lead lands.
S.W. $\frac{1}{4}$.................. 160

39, *Range 2 West.*

Section 2.

Lot 1 & W. $\frac{1}{2}$ of lots 2, 8 &
  4 & E. $\frac{1}{2}$ of lot 6 of N.E. $\frac{1}{4}$·277 61) Thin upland; white oak timber; best qual-
Lots 1, 2 & 3 & E. $\frac{1}{2}$ of lots } ity of lead lands; discoveries made on sur-
  4 & 5 of N.W. $\frac{1}{4}$.........320 } rounding lands constantly.
W. $\frac{1}{2}$ & S.E. $\frac{1}{4}$ of S.E. $\frac{1}{4}$....120
S.W. $\frac{1}{4}$.................. 160

Section 4.

Lot 1 and W. $\frac{1}{2}$ of lot 2 of
  N.E. $\frac{1}{4}$.................. 120) Upland and bottom; timber—oak; well
E. $\frac{1}{2}$ of lot 1 & lots 2, 5 & 6 } watered; north side of river improved; all
  & E. $\frac{1}{2}$ of lots 3 and 4 of } in lead range; on south side of river, farms.
  N.W. $\frac{1}{4}$.................. 881 27
S.W. fr. $\frac{1}{4}$.................. 157 59

Section 10.

N. $\frac{1}{2}$ of section............ 320) Broken upland; well timbered; water, both
S.E. $\frac{1}{4}$.................. 160 } spring and branch; in mineral range.
W. $\frac{1}{2}$ of S.W. $\frac{1}{4}$......... 80

Section 12.

W. $\frac{1}{2}$ of section............ 320 } Broken upland; well timbered; no water;
   } in mineral range.

Section 14.

N. $\frac{1}{2}$ of N.W. $\frac{1}{4}$......... . 80)
N.E. $\frac{1}{4}$.................. 160 } Same.
N. $\frac{1}{2}$ of S.E. $\frac{1}{4}$......... 80

Section 22.

W. $\frac{1}{2}$ & S.E. $\frac{1}{4}$ of N.E. $\frac{1}{4}$...120) Fair upland; well timbered and watered;
S.E. $\frac{1}{4}$.................. 160 } oak; meeting house on N.E. $\frac{1}{4}$; in mineral
W. $\frac{1}{2}$ of S.W. $\frac{1}{4}$......... 80 } range.

Section 24.

W. $\frac{1}{2}$ & N.E. $\frac{1}{4}$ of N.W. $\frac{1}{4}$...120 } Same.
S.W. $\frac{1}{4}$.................. 160

TOWNSHIP.	Area. Acres	100ths.	DESCRIPTIVE NOTES.
Section 26.			
W. ½ of section	320		Broken upland; two small farms on section; in mineral range.
S.E. ¼ of N.E. ¼	40		
S.E. ¼	160		
Section 28.			
N.E. ¼	160		Same; well timbered; varieties of oak; in mineral range.
N.W. fr. ¼	128	12	
E. ½ & N.W. ¼ of S.W. ¼	120		
Section 34.			
W. ½ of N.W. ¼	80		Same.
N.E. ¼	160		
S. ½ of section	320		
Section 36.			
W. ½ & N.E. ¼ of N.W. ¼	120		Same.
S.W. ¼	160		
38, *Range* 2 *West.*			
Section 2.	651	60	Best quality of lead lands.
Section 4.			
Lot 2 & E. ½ of lot 1 of N. E. ¼	125	26	Best quality of lead lands.
Lot 2 of N.W. ¼	81	1	
E. ½ & S.W. ¼ of S.E. ¼	120		
W. ½ & S.E. ¼ of S.W. ¼	120		
Section 10	640		Broken upland; oak timber; mineral lands.
Section 12.			
W. ½ & N.E. ¼ of N.W. ¼	120		Same.
S.W. ¼	160		
Section 14	640		Same.
Section 22	640		Broken upland; improvements on N.E. and S.E. ¼; all in mineral range.
Section 24.			
W. ½ of section	320		Same.
Section 26	640		Best quality of lead lands.
Section 28.			
N. ½ of section	320		Good agricultural lands; well timbered and watered; fine farm on section; best quality of lead lands.
S E. ¼	160		
W. ½ & S.E. ¼ of S.W. ¼	120		
Section 34.			
E. ½ of N.E. ¼	80		Broken white oak lands; best quality of lead lands.
S.E. ¼	160		
E. ½ of S.W. ¼	80		
N.W. ¼ & S.E ¼ of N.W. ¼	80		
Section 36.			
N.W. ¼	160		Same.